Bonjour P[...]
lovely to [...]
at BBB 22
Hope Irving

C000091683

THIS OR THAT

HOPE IRVING

COPYRIGHT

Editing: Sarah TORPEY / **Proofreading**: Eileen PROKSCH
Cover Design: Simon FRANKLIN

❀ Created with Vellum

ABOUT THIS OR THAT

Sometimes, a kiss can knock you out faster than a blow to the head, rendering you unable to think straight.

It shouldn't have happened, but now... all bets are off.
A stranger shoved his tongue down my throat.
A first!
The out-of-place cowboy gave me a taste of my own medicine
after I stole a sloppy kiss in a Parisian club.
I was out of line. He was unapologetic.
My assumed-straight orientation didn't erase how my body
ignited under his touch.

Months later, we're face-to-face again; well, mouth-to-mouth! I
want to hate him. I hate to want him. So much...
Troy Hunter presents two options...
Not an ultimatum, just his favorite game.

This: Forget our differences and explore our attraction, finally
breaking the mold that my oppressive father chose for me.
Or that: Move on and return to safer ground, remaining the good
boy who foolishly believes he's got it all figured out.

Picking one will be a heck of a challenge. For now, we can give in to our insane chemistry. We have an expiration date, so it's better this way.

But in the end, what do we really want?

This or that?

This or That features two hot, indecisive, and playful studs that briefly appear in Omega Artist (A Cocky Hero Club novel). It's your chance to see how it all started for them. This or That is a standalone.

---

*This book was previously part of a charity anthology entitled **Anyone But You**; it was originally published in early 2021. Since then, I've added new content, including a bonus epilogue! Same enemies-to-lovers storyline. Same hot and sweet characters. More focus on certain scenes. Discover or rediscover Mike and Troy's story... Most of all, enjoy this new version!*

CHAPTER 1
I WALK THE LINE

Troy

My fist connects with the bastard's jaw, and even the deafening music can't hide the resulting crack.

Damn, that felt liberating!

I heave a shaky breath, ignoring the pain that radiates from the impact, and wiggle my fisted hand to take the edge off.

Losing his balance, he falls backwards and his muscular body skids across the VIP room's luxurious leather couch. The cartoonish drooping mouths and wide eyes sported by his friends are priceless. Shock. Amusement. Indignation.

"Don't you dare treat my friend like that!" I warn.

Rubbing his cheek, he glowers at me. His dark green eyes capture my chocolate ones, but I remain rooted.

"Go back to your barn, cowboy," he snarls before a smirk forms on his handsome face. Jerk! His unfocused eyes betray his level of intoxication that probably—or hopefully?—caused his misconduct... unless he's the typical entitled clientele that frequents this Parisian club. Damn, I despise abusive people, especially when under the influence!

"Troy?" A feminine voice tears me from my fabricated reaction. "Earth to Troy?"

Because, of course, acting on that fantasy wouldn't be clever. Because, of course, hitting a customer would get me fired from this bartending job and jeopardize my precarious finances. Because, of course, my coworker, Anna, can handle herself just fine around intoxicated pricks like this one. But witnessing their encounter from afar sent a shot of adrenaline. His good looks are a fact, not my opinion. Anyone could attest to that, no matter their sexual orientation. Still, gorgeous or not, I can't stand anyone who doesn't fight fair. It brings back too many childhood memories.

Oblivious to my inner conflict, Anna's fingertips brush the knuckles of my clenched hand, making my shoulders relax and my body shiver. She's not prone to PDA, but when our eyes locked seconds ago, she read the anger that fueled my fantasy. A fantasy where the guy addressed me in his perfect English accent, which would be par for the course, considering the number of tourists that this exclusive venue attracts. A fantasy where the guy commented on my unmistakable hat that my boss insists I wear after foolishly donning it during my interview. A fantasy where the guy noticed more than the aforementioned hat…

"You've zoned out again."

Biting my lower lip with my front teeth, I nod absentmindedly, my eyes on hers, and I'm at a loss for words. It's frightening how she can read me like an open book. What a bummer that there's no attraction there, since we're compatible on so many other levels. Movies: Christian Bale and Christopher Nolan are the best. Books: Jim Harrison and Thomas Harris are our favorites. Music: electro, since she unfortunately loathes country.

"What's up with you? You've been doing that much more lately." I shrug. Instead of supplying an explanation, I share the visual that my mind created. In turn, a hearty peal of laughter erupts from her chest.

"How many times do we need to have this conversation? It's not the first time, and it won't be the last, Troy." Her upturned lips warm my heart. She's right, but I can't wrap my head around it. "What did you expect?" Her big blue eyes shoot me a flippant look. "We work in a club. People dance. People drink. People touch." She pats my toned bicep as she wanders off to attend to other patrons.

Before she's out of earshot, I propose, "Let me handle that table for now, okay?"

Her mane of dark curls bounces in agreement as she departs. We tend to the groups that crowd the trendy venue, tuning the electro music out, no matter how much we love it. Otherwise, the volume would make it impossible to focus on the task at hand.

"By the way, they ordered Dom Pérignon." She winks as she passes me by.

"What? When were you gonna tell me?" She should have communicated this when we discussed my virtual punch, not ten minutes later!

She stops in her tracks, turns my way, and emphasizes the first word playfully. "*Now* is a good time. That hot guy and his grabby hands deserved to cool off a bit. His looks are no excuse!" she declares as she arrives at my side.

As much as I agree with her, clients can't wait. That isn't part of the deal, especially not here. No matter how obnoxious some of them are, we can't let our feelings interfere. I frown. He must have pissed her off more than she let on for her to behave like this. Her palm rests on my right elbow over my black long-sleeved T-shirt. Is she trying to channel my growing irritation? At this guy. At the situation. At her.

"I'll grab the champagne glasses from the back." She raises her voice to be heard over the music. "François will get the Dom for you." She winks at her innuendo and carries on in an even tone. "We'll go together in a minute, okay?"

I grumble my reply, unconvinced. I know the drill, though. Ice in the giant bucket. A napkin to wrap around the neck of the bottle. My mind sets my body in motion.

With that, she flees without further notice. My shoulders tense for no apparent reason. Granted, I pride myself on being independent and despise receiving orders, except from François because he's our boss. But then again, Anna didn't boss me around; she simply suggested that we get moving and finally attend to the whim of wasted rich kids... Kids, who might very well be nearing thirty, so older than me by a few years. Kids, who obviously take their privileged life for granted, like I did over a decade ago. Kids, who will be as despicable as adults as they are now. Thank God, the club doesn't attract many of those.

Why am I so worked-up? My imaginary assault? Anna's surprising behavior? Channing's smirk?

No, this guy and I aren't on a first-name basis and never will be. The nickname's my own doing because, trust me, he's Channing Tatum's spitting image, and fuck, did my dick get the message when he and his snooty friends entered the place. His broad frame. His sex-on-legs demeanor. His gorgeous face. All Channing, and the jackass is well aware of the resemblance. As he is of the fact that all eyes were on him, including mine. I doubt that he registered that my attraction to him was more sexual than Channing-related. How could he? In his eyes, I'm only the help. Period... And now, thanks to the way he treated Anna, I know how he views the staff. Disposable goods. Must be what triggered my fictitious punch to his smug face.

"You're lost in your head again. Come on."

I shake my head to get back to reality and round the bar with the heavy bucket in hand. Making sure she's securely holding the tray and none of the ten glasses risk falling, Anna and I sidestep tables and patrons on our way to the back of the club where the secluded room is situated, separated from the main room by a one-way mirror. In order to provide more privacy, these guests have a personal dance floor.

I hold the VIP room door so that she can deposit the tray on the table without difficulty. The second she straightens her posture and looks my way, Channing mumbles something incoherent, attesting to his drunken state. That makes me question why they ordered three more bottles. Clearly, they've already had more than enough.

Damn, he irritates me!

I plaster a fake smile on my face in return, and my eyes don't leave his as I make quick work of the cork and start pouring the champagne. The liquid effervesces and that's the moment that Channing chooses to, yet again, grope my coworker's plump ass.

What the hell?

My cheeks heat, and I'm thankful that the dim light hides my glare. My blood boils as I debate whether to act on my earlier fantasy.

"Nah, that wouldn't be smart," I scold myself between gritted teeth. I refuse to allow this to go unpunished and resolve to show Channing the error of his ways. For now, I have one word left.

War.

CHAPTER 2
WHEN BAD DOES GOOD

Mike

"You like it, don't you?" I don't recognize my own voice as my question comes out brasher than anticipated.

I'm not sure why the pretty barmaid would come back for round two if she weren't remotely interested. Right?

"Sir, I suggest you remove your hand from my derrière."

Seated—or rather slouched—on the comfortable couch, I register that my hand is glued to her sumptuous ass that's showcased by a fitted black dress. Since the young woman is to the right of the couch, the oversized square coffee table doesn't get in the way.

"Or what?"

My daring tone echoes through the room, and my friends offer a mix of disapproving groans and cheers. Surprisingly enough, the women are the ones encouraging me.

The devil inside my head joins the party. *Of course, she wants more.* The next thing I know, my hand snatches her wrist and yanks her my way, propelling her perky derrière to my lap.

She readjusts her position to keep from falling to the side, and I take that as an invitation. My free hand draws her closer and, without asking for permission, my lips crash against hers in a sloppy kiss. Instead of relaxing into the kiss, my body stiffens, and not because I sport a semi. Nope. Her refusal to open up for me does it. My tongue doesn't have time to coax her into cooperating.

In the blink of an eye, the girl is plucked from my hold by her cowboy knight in all-black, not-so-shining armor. Before I'm able to react, she rushes to the guy's side and lets out a sigh of relief that even I can hear. Loud and clear.

Apparently, she couldn't be happier to hide behind her human shield. "Get off me, you perv!" she shrieks now that she's safe.

My friends' voices become white noise. Me, a perv? The word sends an icy chill down my spine. I beg to differ. Whoever this girl is, she has to come to her senses and fathom that I'm anything but. I may be sloshed, but I felt her attraction to me. Loud and clear.

Flinging myself out of my seat like a Jack-in-the-box on steroids, I notice that the world around me won't stop spinning. Somehow, I manage to make a beeline to the current object of my desire but am blocked by the bartender, who acts as a human shield. Growling, I do a piss-poor job of steadying my antsy body. My anger grows by leaps and bounds, and I inhale deeply. Loud and clear.

As I prepare to exhale, my wrist is circled by potent fingers, flooding my body with warmth… until I realize who they belong to. The bartender twists my arm behind my back while hauling me closer to him.

The fucker's a couple of inches shorter than my 6' 1", but he's undeniably strong. His overbearing eyes meet mine, and my heart jumps into my throat. At this point, the blasting music ceases. My stupid friends vanish. My female temptation disappears.

I stand inches away from the guy, and his hot breath fans

across my face. Too dumbstruck to push him away, my lips part as I silently question his next move.

After counting to three, his hungry mouth slams against mine as I start to stutter, "What the—"

He swallows my words, his lips pressing harder against mine. As absurd as I find his cowboy hat, since we're in Paris, I'm relieved that, paired with the darkness, it surely conceals our lips from prying eyes, considering where we're standing.

My weekend stubble scrapes his clean-shaven face, but he doesn't budge. The foreign sensation sends yet another shiver. By the time I realize that I have a free hand that can be used to push him away, it's too late. He buries his fingers in my short light brown hair, positioning my head to get a better angle. Meanwhile, my caged wrist travels from the small of my back to my butt. Then, the stranger's firm hand tightens and clamps on my ass as if we were alone. Together. Naked. Such an intimate gesture. Such an unexpected gesture. Such a revolting gesture. My sloshed mind can't make sense of what's happening. Talk about a twist of fate!

Against my better judgment, I let his skillful tongue slide into my mouth. Again, the difference of his kiss strikes me. His is demanding. His is unapologetic. His is unprecedented. My heart thumps so hard that I wonder whether I'm about to have a heart attack. I'm no longer interested in my current state, mental or otherwise, and much too horny to stop the startling assault.

My confused brain wonders how long it's been. It feels like it's been hours, although that's impossible. His hold on my hair becomes more forceful, and the back of my neck becomes so stiff that it aches. I don't react.

Soon enough, his tongue brushes against mine. I'm petrified, numb, stunned… but that doesn't deter him. Quite the opposite. He kisses me like his life depends on it, making all kinds of erotic noises that only I can hear and have a direct connection to my cock, no-holds-barred, and all of my rational thoughts short-circuit. My nerve endings go radio silent for a split second when his hand pauses before it resumes squeezing my designer jean-clad flesh… with a vengeance. My previous tensions vanish to settle between my legs.

Oh, fuck! How is this possible?

It takes another second. Another minute. Or is it another hour? To register that my work friends whistle and clap at the searing kiss. They must be as hot and bothered by it as I am.

Wait, what?

This can't be. I'm not gay.

Coming to my senses at last, I wrench my lips from his and manage to free myself from his hold. His kiss. His spell. Instinctively, I take a step back to put some necessary distance between us.

The excitement hasn't subsided, and other nearby patrons break into applause. What the hell is their problem?

Well, as long as nobody comments on my raging erection, I won't punch anyone.

Wait, what?

Of course, I will. A knee-jerk reaction takes over as soon as the words "Get off me, you perv!" leave my mouth, and I slap the cheek that was previously affixed to mine.

What's gotten into me? This sobered me up for good, and I'm just pretending to be plastered as an excuse.

Caressing his cheek, the guy's glaring like I was the one who mauled his mouth, a knowing look flashing on his face. He has some nerve. *What the fuck have I done now?* He assaulted me. He forced his tongue into my mouth. He pressed his semi against my own. At the thought, I clear the lump from my constricted throat.

Dammit, what's wrong with me?

"Yeah, keep telling yourself that I'm the one at fault here." And the fucker cracks up in my face.

Frowning, I take another step back and ram into the arm of

the couch. I ignore the guests' requests for more. I don't want more; what I want is to regain the upper hand. *When did this go wrong?*

The cowboy turns to his coworker and whispers something that I can't hear, which frustrates me to no end. She cups her hand around his ear as she replies, and her back faces me as the revengeful stranger claims, "It was only fair to give you a taste of your own medicine." He lets out a bitter chuckle. "I just didn't expect…" He trails off.

Part of me hopes that he'll admit that he liked it. Heat courses from my head down to my toes, and I will myself to remain calm, although my poker face is out of order, thanks to my alcohol consumption.

Once again, he surprises me by using my words. "You liked it, didn't you?"

Perplexed, my thumb thoughtlessly caresses my swollen lips, but he couldn't care less. He laces his fingers with his coworker's, and I wonder if they are a couple. Nah, he wouldn't have acted so recklessly.

When his hand grasps the doorknob, his head tilts my way. "I know you did." His intense gaze bores into mine and he turns to leave the room. For good this time. He crosses the threshold and declares, "So, what's your choice? This or that?"

Wait, what?

CHAPTER 3
SUNSET LOVER

Troy

My colorful plate contrasts with the gloomy Parisian October weather. Not that I'm sure whether this is typical, since I only got here in June. So far, the weather's been mostly decent. The other students from my exchange program are cool and don't give a flying fuck that I'm here on a scholarship, and my coworkers at the club are awesome. Luckily, all of them speak English, so I couldn't complain since I don't speak much French, although I now understand it pretty well. Granted, it's quite a change from the Dallas-Fort Worth area where I grew up, or New York where I've lived for years, but I'm having a blast.

"The croissant's mine!" I bat Anna's sneaky hand away and smile. "If you want one, go get one. After all, it's an all-you-can-eat brunch. It's one of the perks of this place, on top of the trendy vibes and beautiful people."

She groans at my sarcastic remark. The Canal Saint-Martin is all that, fashionable and full of people that the French refer to as *bo-bo*, but we Americans would call hipsters. Although it's much more enjoyable when it's warmer, the promenade and area are simply unique. Trendy furniture stores. Trendy vegan cafés. Trendy boutiques... Did I mention that the Canal was trendy and I'm not surprised that Dutch Anna chose it? "Nah, I'm not supposed to eat stuff like that," she whines, giving me her best impression of Puss in Boots.

"Oh, come on! Considering the size of the pastry, I'd say that your agency should require that you have at least two." I stare at my plate, then back at my friend. "It's so tiny." I grab a knife and slice it horizontally before slathering it with Nutella for good measure.

Anna's dark blue eyes widen as she watches me with envy, licking her full lips. She takes a sip of her green tea after polishing off her bowl of mixed fruit and granola. Her dark shoulder-length hair sways to the rhythm of the background music that I don't recognize. "Are we going to discuss last night's..."—she takes a look around, thoughtful—"incident?"

Stuffing the pastry into my mouth as a delay tactic, I gulp it in two bites. "What do you mean?" It's my turn to lick my lips so that I don't waste any of the delicious Nutella. What I'm not telling her is that I'll work out twice as hard as soon as I get back to my place, near Bastille, another area that's popular with the younger crowd, thanks to its number of popular bars.

"Oh, please, Troy. You know exactly what I mean..." Her body leans across the table, and she whispers, "Or rather, *who!*" Her hand finds the top of my messy dark copper curls and ruffles them.

When she withdraws her hand and focuses on her food, I pick at my cuticle, unsure of what she expects me to say. "Listen, I really think that there's nothing left to say. That jerk at the club scared you, although I would never have guessed his behavior would have such an impact on you. You asked me to drive you back home like you do whenever you don't want to be alone. I spent the night like I do whenever you ask me to. We fucked like we do whenever we feel like it. End of story." With that, my eyes go back to the task at hand, and I concentrate on the remainder of my now cold spinach omelet.

"I'm well aware of those facts. I was there, remember?" She makes a *tssk* noise to underline her disapproval. "As I am of our friends with benefits agreement... and thank you for scratching my itch, by the way." She giggles. "It was very... pleasurable."

"In case I wasn't noisy enough, the pleasure was mutual, Anna." I clean up most of what's left on my plate.

Yeah, it's too bad that she's not my type and vice-versa. It would make things so much easier for both of us. I wouldn't have to play the part of the fake boyfriend whenever her parents are around, for one, simply because they can't comprehend why she's still single. Apparently, her mom—also a model, back in the day—had no difficulties with her bank account or with finding "appropriate" suitors from which to choose a husband. Anna's not that lucky, so she works at the club to make ends meet but keeps it a secret. As far as men are concerned, she's unwilling to tie the knot with a wealthy guy who's solely after her appearance. That's how I ended up in the picture. But then again, I'm not looking for a relationship right now. I love my freedom too damn much. Thank God, Anna and I both know where the other stands.

I feel the weight of her gaze and look her way. Figuring out what's on her mind isn't rocket science, so I stop toying with her. She's a good friend and I have no intention of ruffling her feathers.

I make a point to not stare at her when I ask, "Kissing that guy is what's bothering you, right?"

"You bet!"

I take a bite and chew slowly to give me a moment to think, toying with my food rather than finishing it. My eyes were bigger than my stomach. Leaning back in my chair, I wait with a smirk on my face.

"What got into you? Why did you do that?" The fact that she

can't even say it aloud speaks volumes. At once, I can't help but wonder if she's happy that I interrupted her misfortune, disgusted that I sucked face with a stranger, or aroused because the stranger happened to be a very fuckable guy.

"Would you rather…" I chuckle at one of my favorite expressions. "Would you rather,"— I repeat, my tone more assertive this time—"nail a random hot chick or screw your father's best friend?"

"What does that have to do with anything?" Asking this, she can't help but smile, well aware of my favorite game.

"So, hot girl or Dad's friend? Which is it? This or that?"

"That." She lets out a throaty chortle, and her eyes get a faraway look as she contemplates the idea. I don't have time to inquire further. "I guess." She trails off, obviously perplexed as to where this is heading. A sip of tea later, she confirms, fidgeting in her seat, "I'm into guys, so sex with a girl is out of the question for me."

I raise my brows. "I never specified the aforementioned best friend's gender, mind you. I did say 'hot chick,' though."

"Look, I know some friends who kissed a girl like it was a rite of passage. That's simply not me. I need to be attracted to the person, and women don't do it for me." Her tone is matter-of-fact and way too serious for my taste.

I shoot her a quizzical look. "It's a game, Anna. There's no need to be so square."

"I may be boring according to your standards, but I repeat: hot or not, trust me, I'd rather bang my dad's buddy... The fact that he's a real person shows that your ridiculous game is biased, as always, my friend!"

Rather than reassure her that she isn't boring in bed, I stick out my tongue.

"Ha-ha, that's mature of you, Troy." She swats my hand like a scolding mother, then winks, a mischievous glimmer in her blue eyes. "And don't think that I haven't noticed your lame attempt to ditch my question."

"I'm really not. That's the whole point of my this or that question, to clue you in to what got into me yesterday. Apart from saving your virtue, that is, since I'm well aware that you're a big girl and can handle yourself just fine."

"Carry on, I'm intrigued." Her elbows land on the wooden table while her hands support the weight of her overthinking head. She coughs lightly, then adds, "Actually, what I'm curious about is the fact that you kissed *a guy... him...* so... passionately. Believe me, everyone in that room was turned-on!"

A devilish roar of laughter follows. I'm pleased that the kiss had the expected effect, but I need her to realize that it was more than an impulsive gesture. "What got into me last night was *this*." Air quote again. "In other words, I'd pick nailing a willing hunk anytime." I plaster the most innocent smile on my not so angelic face. *This* is my answer to the *this or that* question. *This* is why I didn't think before acting last night. *This* is where we differ. "Also, I would avoid my parents and their toxic friends like the plague, as you know." Not long after Anna and I clicked, I confessed that I'd been raised by my dad's younger sister for most of my teenage years and left Texas the first chance I got. Only I didn't disclose the reason why I'd been kicked out of their house. Became nonexistent to them. Cut out of their will. That's no one's business.

Anna's eyes linger on our joined hands, and she offers a sheepish smile.

"No need to be sorry, Anna. I was the moron who brought them up in our little game." The palm of my free hand strikes my forehead. "Duh!" Once my hand is back on the table, I joke, "Anyway, what I meant to say was that kissing him to demonstrate that unsolicited attention isn't welcome was too damn tempting. Maybe I was secretly hoping that it would unlock our own private Magic Mike show!" I wiggle my eyebrows, and we both chortle at that. The guy sure looked like Channing Tatum, so it would've been fitting.

Soon after, Anna's jaw drops so low, it's almost comical. It takes a minute for her to process that tidbit.

"The jackass needed to have a taste of his own medicine!" I declare between gritted teeth as my heart races. "So, yeah, I shamelessly kissed the sexy bastard." I hesitate before disclosing a troubling fact. "The perk was that it was a damn good kiss." I heave a happy sigh when I think back to the sensation of his mouth on mine. Goosebumps appear, and I'm glad that my clothes hide my reaction. "And must I remind you that, to my utter surprise, he gave in without much of a fight? It's obvious that he enjoyed it." I pause, willing my mind to stop fantasizing about what it could have been, but won't ever be. Still, I can't help concluding, "A damn good kiss that felt like an appetizer to revenge sex!"

Anna's brows knit in confusion. "You're... you're..." She can't finish her sentence, and her hold on my hand loosens. I need to come clean. I probably should have disclosed this information before we engaged in any kind of relationship beyond friendship. I'm reluctant because, to me, it doesn't make a difference. I hope it'll be the same for her; I do care for her. My throat constricts as I utter the word that my narrow-minded family never understood, causing so much drama.

"Bi."

CHAPTER 4
JUST BREATHE

Mike

My tongue's heavy, and my mouth is as dry as cotton. With my head buried beneath the covers in my expensive bachelor pad in the 6th arrondissement, I shiver at the unpleasant sensation. My place is closer to the Sorbonne than I wish, and it brings an unwanted crowd—mostly preppy students and inquisitive tourists—especially on weekdays. Today, I'm too out of it to notice.

As I debate whether to pry myself out of bed for some water, an arm that doesn't belong to me assaults my muscular chest over the comforter. To add insult to injury, a snore that rivals a chainsaw follows. At that, heat flares down my spine and I growl, wondering if this is a nightmare. Of course, I must be imagining things!

I don't remember bringing anyone home. I don't remember banging anyone. What I do remember, though, now that I'm partially awake, is my dream.

A surprising cowboy hat. An enticing scent. A scorching kiss.

Instantly, the pad of my thumb grazes my lower lip, and I'm hard as a rock. This time, the warmth that courses underneath my skin is of a different nature. My thirst is forgotten when a new hunger takes over.

Good morning, wood!

I roll on my back, lick my palm, and mindlessly slide my hand into my boxer briefs to palm my erection. It's in desperate need of release… and attention.

Keeping my eyes shut, I apply the perfect pressure while letting the lingering dream lead the way. The more I caress my length, the more ragged my breathing becomes.

Holy shit!

Yeah, yeah, my thoughts are profound when I'm jacking off and my mind's on overdrive.

Before my body goes lax, a fleeting thought crosses my mind: no woman will ever have the full roadmap for the perfect hand-job. They think they do. As eager as some are to stroke, suck, and swallow, they don't have a fucking clue about what goes on in a man's body.

Don't get me wrong, I'm twenty-seven and, over the years, I've nailed my fair share of women. Initially, I was too green to pay attention. Later, I believed that it was caused by a stale routine; at least, that's what sex with your high-school sweetheart at an early age will teach you. Part of me was relieved when Ella dumped me after our four-year relationship. The other half was angry that I didn't see it coming.

Then, I began experimenting. All colors, shapes, and sizes. Deep down, I knew I was searching for a meaningful relationship, but first, I had to investigate what I preferred. How I preferred it. Why I preferred it. I learned so much about my body over the next few years. So far, the sentiments that are supposed to accompany a relationship are nowhere to be found. Not that I mind; I'm young and in no rush. Since the crushing breakup, I've decided to concentrate on my new career. From criminal lawyer, like daddy dearest, to fashion design intern to walk in my grandma's shoes. But let's not get into that now.

Focus, Clayton.

I sigh and do just that, pumping with renewed purpose. In the back of my mind, I catalog the women I've met so far. They were good, but not perfect. Don't they say that if you want something done right, do it yourself? That doesn't mean that I want to end up alone; I sure don't.

I snicker at the next question that pops into my head. *Do I have any idea of what women experience when my thumb is circling their clit?* The answer's still no, but I show them a good time or they wouldn't ask for a repeat, right?

Distracted by my runaway thoughts, my free hand roams to my aching balls. Stroking. Cajoling. Pinching. Yeah, no woman's ever touched my family jewels this way. Hell, they rarely do, even when I voice my needs. Like they're scared of them. Like touching them would damage my baby-making potential. Like that's their one and only purpose.

Oh well, I know how to work my body to achieve a quick, powerful, and messy release.

The porn clip that unfolds in my mind is pretty similar to the one that I watched the other day; I enjoy the ones produced by Brandon Boner. The graphic scenes combine with the overwhelming heat from my X-rated dream. This time, a cowboy hat hides the woman's face.

Who cares if it isn't real? My vivid fantasy does the job. The details are fuzzy, but it's enough to get myself off. I wet my lips as my heartbeat accelerates, but I nonetheless try to milk the high. (Pun intended!) My mind remains fixated on the damn cowboy hat, and I urge my imagination to uncover the face that my twisted brain keeps hidden. To no avail.

On the verge of an orgasm, I skillfully handle myself; it's both aggressive and gentle. A satisfied smile lifts the corner of my mouth as pleasure continues to build from deep inside. My thoughts become incoherent while one last question crosses my mind: *How can a woman truly comprehend what goes on between me and my manhood?*

My entire body stiffens and my legs spread wider as I stroke myself like a madman. Next thing I know, the caveman side of me takes over and groans when the climax hits like a tidal wave. "Ohhhh, fuuuuck!"

At once, my heart rate reaches record speed and my eyes pop open. I huff and puff in a feeble attempt to catch my breath as I blow my load on my stomach with such force that the sticky covers plaster to my spent body. The face behind my fantasy stays a blur, but what do I care anyway?

Have I ever come so hard?

"The least you could do is be discreet!"

What?

My head swivels at the unknown feminine voice so quickly that my neck hurts. I forgot that I had company, and it caught me off guard.

My mumble is barely audible, thanks to my groggy sexed-up tone. "At least, I'm not hearing voices," I reply to the gorgeous sleepyhead, who launches the comforter in my direction before lying on her side, elbow on the mattress, her head supported by her manicured nails.

Puzzled, she scrutinizes me. "What?" Our eyes lock in mutual bewilderment. There are so many emotions and unanswered questions in her green eyes that my head spins. *What is she doing here when I mostly hook up at their place? What happened last night? What's her name again? The one with the cowboy hat I dreamt of?*

"Nah, I don't picture you wearing a cowboy hat," I state for my own sake, and I don't miss the tinge of regret in my voice. Could cowgirls be my new thing? Interesting.

She rolls over and sits up, covering her ample breasts as soon as she sees my gaze focus on them. Well, they look too perfect to be real anyway, and as much as I enjoy an impressive rack, I prefer them *au naturel.*

"You're not making any sense, Mike."

"Duh!" I've been lost inside my head almost ever since I woke up.

"Never mind." She heaves an irritated sigh, staring at my flaccid cock that is unfortunately in plain view. Suddenly shy, I reach for the comforter to conceal myself and place my hands behind my head to stay still. "I can't decide if I'm happy that you finally managed to get it up or pissed because I'm not the reason behind it." She looks me in the eye, biting the corner of her lip.

I'm afraid to inquire how she ended up here. Trying to focus on the events that led to this is useless. My exhaustion hasn't subsided, although I'm blissed-out from the fantastic orgasm that she had no part in, and sadly acknowledging the upcoming headache that's slowly but surely taking hold. "I can't decide whether I'm pissed at you for lying about rising to the occasion or happy that you let me take care of myself without interrupting since you were…" I mimic her, scratching my neck while thinking of a witty comeback. Nothing comes to mind. "Since you favored your beauty sleep over sex."

My comment makes her bolt out of bed, taking the comforter with her, and she rolls it around her body, leaving me stark naked. "Listen, Magic Mike." I grumble at the nickname that I despise, even though it's due to my striking resemblance to Channing Tatum when my hair's cut short, which I can't complain about. "I've had enough negativity for now. I'm gonna go make some strong coffee, and we'll have a coherent conversation like grown-ups. So far, you've been anything but magic!" Instead of strolling out of the bedroom, she treads toward the bed and strikes with a bossy command. "Meanwhile, get a hold of yourself. Take a shower and get cleaned up. I hope it'll help clear your mind. Also, friendly reminder: my name's Lisa. The woman you undoubtedly used to show that you had your shit together. The woman you brought home but were too trashed to fuck. The woman you wanted to wear a cowboy hat to remind you of the blistering kiss a stranger stole from you last night. Well, guess what, pretty boy? You don't deserve me."

I'm too stupefied to utter a word. Could she be telling the truth? Why don't I remember a thing? A cold shiver runs down my spine as I try to make sense of her revelations. She's right, I don't deserve her. Since when have I become such an asshole?

She shrugs, her eyes piercing me defiantly. "Considering what you said a minute ago, I bet you jerked off with a cowboy hat in mind. Am I right?"

Incapable of lying, I chuckle while my body breaks out in goosebumps.

Amused by my reaction, she declares, "See, I may be blonde, but don't judge a book by its cover." She secures the covers around her body before they slide down. Too bad, I would have enjoyed the view. "What I don't get, though, is why you brought me back home when it's crystal clear that I wasn't who you wanted. I guess the alcohol's to blame." She looks away for a moment, her fingers caressing her chin. I'm about to interrupt, but she beats me to it. "Unless the alcohol boosted the cowboy's effect?"

"What on earth are you talking about?"

"Last night's encounter? The person wearing a cowboy hat? Ring a bell?" She giggles and I frown, hoping that my frustration isn't too evident. "Interesting that your mind has no recollection, but your body says otherwise." Her mockery compounds my discomfort. "Watching you guys kiss made the other patrons horny! Funny no one figured out how much you enjoyed it. Even your common sense refuses to acknowledge it. Alcohol lowered your inhibitions; that's all I can think of. Too bad it didn't play in my favor…"

After listening to the assumptions that she voiced aloud, I clear my throat, perplexed.

"Calm your tits, Lisa! I probably shouldn't have drank so much. Everything's foggy. I *do* remember a kiss and a cowboy hat. Apparently, you weren't the one wearing it, so now I'm confused. It's like I blacked out." At my honest admission, she sits on the bed and pecks my forehead.

"Sounds like it. And no, the cowboy hat doesn't belong to me. To set the record straight,"—she giggles, which somehow grates on my nerves—"it belongs to…" She trails off.

"Will you stop it already? Spit it out!" I hate that my mind is blank. "Did I stick my inebriated tongue down some married woman's throat and make a fool of myself or what?"

"Nah, no married woman was involved…" Now, that's a relief! But the fact that she trailed off again irks me. "You're not paying attention!" My brow spikes up, silently pleading for the last bit of information. "I said 'you guys.'" She wiggles her eyebrows, teasing me, which in turn, propels me to snatch the covers back from her to hide beneath… because her answer floors me.

"The bartender."

CHAPTER 5
FREE

Troy

"Again, sorry about the last-minute booking, Hunter," my boss for the next fifteen days repeats. He's pretty laid-back, but this issue stresses him out. I can't figure out why.

"Like I said, I'm here and thrilled about it." My smile widens.

The chance landed on my Parisian doorstep in the form of Nicolas Demeulenaere. The infamous Belgian event planner specializes in launching and promoting what I call hipster brands and recently acquired an electro label. Anna introduced us a while back, and when I learned that he was looking for fresh talent, I jumped at his offer. He selected *me* to entertain the patrons on this cruise from Marseille to Rio. How cool is that?

Prior to booking my services, he listened to my tracks on SoundCloud and attended several of my performances. Gigs that were set in France, Belgium, and Spain. Gigs that I managed to juggle while working part-time at the club and studying in Paris full-time. Gigs that ultimately snowballed into something bigger, and my alter ego DJ Monster Hunter became my focus once my internship was over.

And voilà! Here I am two months later. Eight months after I confessed my sexual preference to my friend with benefits. Over twelve months after I landed in Paris.

Monster Hunter isn't the most original name, I'll give you that. Believe it or not, I chose it carefully. On top of the this or that games that I play on a regular basis, I'm also known for my odd sense of humor. What can I say? I found it humorous to attach the judgmental nickname my parents gave me to the last name we have in common. To them, I was a monster. Isn't it ironic that I'm a pretty famous one? Deal with that, bigots!

"You got everything you need?" He lights up a cancer stick without bothering to ask if I mind.

Well, let's see… I'm getting paid to do a job I love, have my travel expenses covered, and might very well snag a deal with his label before the boat arrives in Rio. Oh, and let's not forget the cruise is for singles only! That means I can score easy pussy or willing dick; messing with the customers is even part of the plan. After all, I'm on the rebound after Anna and I decided to terminate our friends with benefits arrangement that our mutual friends dared to call a relationship. Whatever we had at first— carefree, passionate, and unbridled sex—became flavorless over time. We agreed that we were too young to overlook the lack of passion between us… What's the point in having a friend with benefits when there are none, right? She may have also hinted that she was looking for something more meaningful. When we met, we became fast friends. Now, I'm a bit lost. Despite the fact that I know it's the right decision. Despite the fact that we text almost every day. Despite the fact that we became like brother and sister. I mean, what you'd expect from siblings, aside from my own. This change of scenery is perfect…

What is there to complain about?

"Sure do." I ignore his nasty habit; we're outside, and the

smoke stays away for the most part. I haven't seen much of Nicolas since we embarked and am glad we bumped into each other. Standing with our elbows over the railing, we're not quite facing each other, mesmerized by the ocean between Barcelona and tomorrow's destination, Malaga. I stifle a sigh and feel the weight of his stare.

"You okay?" he inquires and waits for me to carry on.

This cruise might land me the deal that I've been waiting for. My pulse quickens at the mere thought. His cigarette isn't what's bothering me, rather the lingering doubt that coils around my insides. I can't meet his eyes for the longest time. He smokes in silence until I say my piece. I clear my constricted throat in hopes it'll keep my tone in check. "Tonight's gonna be the real test."

Barely dressed people come and go behind our backs in a scene reminiscent of spring break. The website mentioned that it was reserved for people under thirty and all sexual orientations were welcome. I snickered at that, knowing full well that most of my gay friends prefer strictly gay events. Who was I to criticize their marketing skills? If I can work and meet people who are as sexually open as I am, that's icing on the cake!

We remain undisturbed by the rowdy voices behind us. It's happy hour, and the bartending staff concocts a wide variety of cocktails for the occasion. I enjoy being on the other side of the fence this time. Bartending at the club has been great, but this is my dream career. This is why I studied business. This is what my future will be if Nicolas gives me the extra push to rise above the noise.

"Why do you say that?"

"Well, the first night was a huge success." He nods at my matter-of-fact words. "It could've been beginner's luck, you know."

"It's funny," he replies, patting my well-defined bicep through my denim jacket. It's May, but the ocean combined with the speed of the ship make evenings downright chilly. "You never struck me as doubtful."

"Oh, I'm not!" I know I'm talented. If not, he wouldn't have spotted me in the first place. "I have to be on top of my game. Patrons are demanding, and I'm not the only DJ on board. There's a reason why they call this Coachella on the Sea..." I trail off, not quite remembering what the website labeled it. "I want to be the best. I want my music to set the ideal mood for their hookups or soulmate scouting." I snicker at that since it's a foreign notion for me. "Keeping it fresh every time I perform is quite a challenge, don't you think?"

"You're right." He takes a pull on his cigarette, then shrugs. "But you know what you're doing."

We make small talk about how his label is expanding, and he eventually mentions that this venue is new to him. Shortly after, he redirects the conversation to my musical influences. I can't deny that country music is a huge part of my life as well. Wearing a cowboy hat as a trademark makes that fairly obvious, but he's interested in electro, not country singers.

"Come on, let's go toast to your success!" Without waiting for an answer, he herds me towards the massive bar. Everything's larger than life on this ship. The bars. The clubs. The pools. "It'll loosen your nerves," he declares as we clink our champagne glasses.

The conversation flows, and I nod at regular intervals to prove that he has my full attention. He's as passionate about his job as I am about my music. We're on our second glass when I discern that he also has a passion for fumbling his man bun.

He must notice my stare—or he's a gifted mind-reader—because he snorts before saying, "It's not my favorite look either!" He winks knowingly. "I have to look a certain way in my line of work." He shrugs. "I should get rid of it." His sentence comes out as a question and I'm so baffled that I keep quiet. "Right?" he presses.

I gulp what's left of my beverage to buy some time. "You're asking the wrong person, Nicolas. I'm not here to judge or give advice on a hairstyle," I force myself to reply, fidgeting.

"Not asking for either, but your opinion is welcome."

"Is this a test?" I ask warily. It's a lose-lose situation. If I tell him that he looks great, he'll think that I'm kissing his ass. If I don't, he'll think that I'm an ungrateful prick. Damn, I loathe these types of situations.

"I value honesty is all. No test."

Why? Why me? Why now? I can't tell him that I'm confused as to why he's obligated to change his appearance to play the part. Not that it's bad, but the forty-something man is a force to be reckoned with in his field whether he wears one or not.

Marching towards the bar again, but for water to clear my head this time, we remain quiet for a bit. I quench my thirst while his eyes focus on me. Once again, he doesn't press the issue and opts for another route.

My discomfort hasn't subsided. "If you're not happy with it, you should get rid of it. You should be the one to rule your life, not your job or anything else. That's my two cents."

"See, that wasn't so hard, was it? Thank you."

"Glad I could help," I joke before informing him that I should get ready for my set.

He waves goodbye. "I'll see you in a bit, Hunter."

On the way to my cabin, I dwell on our exchange. He can't know that I despise restrictive boxes and typecasting. I'm not twenty-five yet, but I'm already way past that. I won't pretend to be someone I'm not to please others... That doesn't mean that I'm disrespectful or try to impose my views, rather that I detest being told who I should be. By peer pressure. By unspoken rules. By a narrow-minded society.

He called me Hunter, like others have done in the past. But tonight, it makes me think of Mr. and Mrs. Hunter, the two individuals who gave me life.

Refusing to conform to their definition of the perfect son is what instigated our first argument, which was followed by countless others that tore our family apart for no valid reason, if you ask me. As the oldest of five, I was expected to rightfully inherit the prominent family-owned business. It seems that my parents didn't appreciate finding me lip-locked with one of my buddies and couldn't care less that it was in the privacy of my bedroom that they entered without warning. It seems that my parents couldn't fathom that kissing a boy didn't automatically translate to their son being a so-called faggot, not that it should matter anyway. It seems that my parents couldn't accept that being bi was a thing, not a pretense to avoid being labeled gay. Yup, I've always been attracted to a person, not a specific gender, and hadn't fathomed it would be an issue. To them, it was. They shamed me. They called me names. They spread hate. In turn, it led to my eviction from the family home and financial support over ten years ago. My brothers and sisters might resent me for refusing to comply, but I wouldn't know since I lost touch with all of them.

Anyway, enough of that trip down memory lane. Today is a good day, and I refuse to let this sour my mood.

No matter how hard I try, with each passing hour, I grow more restless. I can't make sense of why this upcoming event is affecting me this way. Wolfing down my dinner at record speed doesn't help my stomach, which is already in knots.

Once I'm behind my station setting up the first mix, I'm finally able to relax. My shoulders aren't so stiff. My chest isn't so tight. My legs aren't so wobbly. I've got this.

Let's get this show on the road.

ASAP.

CHAPTER 6
FORTUNATE SON

Mike

"Did you hear a word I said?" Pacing the room, an exasperated sigh escapes my mouth. There's a grumble at the other end of the line. "What was I thinking? Of course, you didn't *hear*..." My annoyance grows. "Because first, you'd have to *listen*, and you never do."

"Watch your tone, son." His proverbial bitterness makes a comeback.

Can't blame it on the early hour on your side of the ocean, since you're already at work with your minions!

Criminal law will do that to you, he claims. I've lost interest in finding out for myself. I've lost interest in trying to please the despot. I've lost interest in contorting to his vision of the perfect son. To this day, I have no clue what my mother saw in him. Granted, they were young and set up by their parents for the sole purpose of producing an heir for a privileged Bostonian lineage. A marriage that fell apart within a couple of years. A baby that arrived too late to save it. An accident that labeled me as weak and hasted my disgrace in my father's rigid view.

Fuck my life!

Magnus, the Scandinavian GQ look-alike. We instantly became friends, and I'll be his best man next month.

"It'd do you some good to give up on this ridiculous whim. Get your life back together. Make your mother and me proud." His statement is delivered so casually that it takes me a second to wrap my head around it. A bead of sweat trickles down my forehead as I process his comment. Time and time again, I've explained that I decided to follow Grandma Lizzie's passion; no matter how wealthy my grandma was, she favored designing and sewing my mom's clothes for a unique wardrobe and perfect fit.

Save your breath, Clayton.

A witty comeback is useless, and we're miles apart anyway. I groan nonetheless, pissed that he brought up my mom, although they aren't on speaking terms. She's the one person who's stood by my side every step of the way. It doesn't make a difference that we haven't connected lately—stupid time zones!—she *is* proud of me.

"Okay, Dad," I agree, knowing full well that he disapproves of the word he considers a term of endearment. I mutely count to three, assuming he'll cut me off. When he doesn't, I continue, "I'll text you to confirm the appointment when I'm ready to board the plane." With my half-lie, he wishes me a good trip, which is probably one of the nicest things he's said in months.

Fuck my life!

Tossing my phone on the bed, I fix myself two more cups of coffee that I guzzle as soon as they're done, convinced that the hot beverage will keep me awake for what's to come. They numb my taste buds, so that's one step in the right direction. Next, I need a shower to rinse away the filth that my father hurled my way over the last half hour. Hence, I do so, my mind clouded with dark thoughts.

I have to brace myself for what's to come. One way or another, right?

I press too hard while shaving and cut myself. Again, too

numb to bother, I carry on with my routine, preoccupied with how the evening unfolded thus far.

Being the trooper that I am, I managed to play nice during dinner and entertain my four friends who constitute the bachelor party, including the soon-to-be-wed Matteo. Poker Face Mike is a master at concealing his boredom on this floating prison.

I inwardly berate Simon, Magnus, and James for choosing this venue. My Italian best friend will be marrying Luana in Rio in less than two weeks. Why they decided to have their closest friends embark on two different singles cruises is beyond me. The days are dragging; it's like being stuck in *Groundhog Day*. Eat. Drink. Sunbathe. Party. Fuck. Sleep. Repeat. At least, the girls are either as bored as I am or desperate enough to be agreeable. It gives a temporary reprieve from the monotony, yet I'm eager to break the curse I've carried since I was born, an inability to find true love that lasts.

I need to try harder to get out of my slump, fast. Granted, I can't seem to find anyone that holds my interest, but I will find my person.

"Right?" It's a rhetorical question, but delivered out loud, as if to convince myself that tonight's going to be different.

Absentmindedly, I grab my iPhone from the bed and scroll through my contacts with my thumb, then press my best friend's number.

"Yo!" His greeting is garbled, which tells me that I must've woken him up.

If I'd known, I would have ditched the electro gig altogether, but they insisted that the guy's a rising star. So, instead, I hear myself say, "I'll be on the upper deck in five."

When I eventually get there, I stop in my tracks, flabbergasted by the odd sea of people. Squinting to spot my buddies, I brace myself and join them. "So, the gig's outside," I state the obvious like the moron I am, although I now remember Matteo saying that it was in the open for once. They nod in unison. The music's blasting; they might not have heard a word I said. Oh well…

Each has a cup in hand; I should've hit the bar first. What was I thinking coming here anyway? Why didn't I ask more questions when Matteo mentioned the upper deck? I take in the scene and do my best to suppress my sour mood. They're all crammed together, lolling their heads in the direction of the stage, shuffling their feet to the repetitive rhythm. Not dancing!

"How long have you guys been here?" I greet my buddies with a friendly pat on the shoulder. Glee is evident on their stupid faces, so I plaster a fake smile on mine.

"A while," is all I get from the ever-chatty Simon as we all approach the robotic crowd.

They briefly comment on the movie they continued after I left Matteo's cabin to take my dreaded phone call.

"I like Monster's sound," Matteo declares, raising his voice to be heard over what I'd refer to noise, which I keep to myself. Monster? Whatever… I already regret agreeing to this as I watch them mimic the others, as if in a trance. So I pretend to be as high as the rest of them to conceal my grumpiness. In truth, the music isn't awful, just not my thing; I'm more of a classic rock or Motown kind of guy.

The DJ says something that I can't decipher. The guests complain about it, but I couldn't care less.

"I'm gonna grab a drink. Anyone want one?" I gesture towards their cups that must be empty by now. They shake their heads, fascinated by the atmosphere of the show. I shrug.

A few minutes later, I wait in line in front of the expansive bar. What's so special about this Monster guy anyway? "This is ridiculous," I rant between gritted teeth.

On my way back to my friends, a guy bumps my arm, nearly knocking the cup out of my hand. "Hey, watch where you're going, asshole!"

"Hunter!" Swiveling his head in the direction of the girl's

voice instead of paying attention to me, said asshole blocks the way and watches her weave through the crowd. "Your hat!"

Riled-up by his carelessness, I'm about to give him a piece of my mind. Not that he'll care, since he has the audacity to pull her to him, snake his arm around her waist, and bend her into a deep Hollywood-style kiss with a whole lot of tongue. Who does he think he is?

When they come up for air, I sneer as she lovingly places his hat over his wayward hair. My eyes bug. My face falls. My pulse races.

I can't utter a word. The fucker smirks, holding my gaze. The realization slowly dawns on me.

How is this possible?

With this unlikely reunion, my disoriented cock hardens, remembering the effect he had on me. Our forbidden kiss. His cowboy hat. My wet dream.

Him!

CHAPTER 7
BASIC INSTINCT

Troy

"You've got to be kidding me!" I joke, letting go of clingy Mallory. The weight of her stare doesn't escape me, and I incline my head to insinuate that she shouldn't stick around. The perceptive girl complies; from our brief time together, she knows better than to argue.

Good! This is between Channing and me.

My brow quirks. "Small world, huh?" I taunt. Welcoming the breeze after spending hours on stage, I wipe my forehead with the sleeve of my denim jacket.

The rest of the world, no matter how small, ceases to exist. Simply because what are the odds, right?

Should I be grateful or resentful at the trick that the universe is playing on us? Taking him in, I decide on the former. The guy's as gorgeous as I remember. My attention is drawn to his sensual lips, and his green eyes bore into mine. The tip of his tongue darts out, licking his plump lower lip. Transfixed, I'm hurtled back to the club where I kissed him months ago. The taste. The softness. The fervor. He resisted, then leaned into the kiss that I stole from him. With that, my neck stiffens and so does my shaft.

Great!

Now I'm sporting a semi while ogling this beautiful stranger from the past. I can't deny that his handsome face is part of the appeal and probably why I continue to be affected after all this time. Seeing him in the flesh, I'm swamped with a surge of conflicted sensations. I don't believe in signs, but I'm an opportunist. It's what landed me on this ship; I might as well take advantage of it.

It's time to put some distance between us and the dancing zombies, bopping in unison to a recording that I put on during my break. Do they even care that I'm not live on stage?

For now, I couldn't care less. I'm not sure what I want from him, but I refuse to let him escape quite yet. We have some sort of unfinished business to attend to. Pent-up anger. Maybe I'd like him to own up to acting like a jerk. Conflicted feelings. Maybe I'd like to kiss him again to flush him out of my system. Sinful thoughts. Maybe I'd like him to confess to enjoying the kiss as much as I did.

"We need to talk." My tone is adamant, and I snatch his elbow to escort him away from the crowd. I expect him to refuse or argue, but he does neither; maybe he does want to say his piece. His longer legs give the false impression that he's leading when I'm guiding the way. Entertained by how compliant Channing is, I bite the inside of my cheek to keep my big mouth shut. He grunts, which boosts my horniness. I try to remain calm. He needs to come to terms with the situation by the time that we reach my destination of choice.

A fleeting thought makes me question his sexual orientation; maybe he hit on Anna because he was drunk or closeted. For all I know, he may very well be bi because I clearly affect him, which pleases me immensely. My throat is parched as I debate where to begin. Passing the bar, he stops, guzzles his beverage in record time, and deposits the empty cup on the counter.

His eyes focus on the ground when he asks in a shaky voice, "Where to?" He looks both lost and determined. There's something about him that intrigues me, and I'm not talking about his lips that glisten with whatever quenched his thirst. Something I felt in Paris, although his attitude had been less than honorable.

Curious, I behave myself and tilt my head in the direction of a relatively secluded corner. High on our proximity, I once again ignore the rush of warmth that unfurls in my chest. My breathing becomes progressively more ragged. I don't give a shit if he calls me out on it.

"So?" he says simply, turning to face me, remaining a safe distance from the wall. His jaw clenches, and he crosses his muscular arms over his chest in defiance.

Or protection?

Speechless, I let out a breath that I didn't realize I was holding while I witness the utter confusion flash across his gorgeous face. "I won't apologize," I blurt.

One second, he's shooting daggers, and the next, his pupils dilate; drugs have nothing to do with it.

So much for keeping your emotions at bay, pretty boy!

I can't make sense of it, but he doesn't give me time to make heads or tails of the situation. As if registering that he's let his guard down, he closes his eyes, preventing me from interpreting anything more. When his eyes pin me again, his face is impassive.

Did I dream his reaction to me? Nahhh, can't be…

I take a step towards him. He doesn't flinch.

What's going on inside that head of yours? Are you bi-curious, then?

"I never asked you to." The beads of sweat collecting on his forehead prove that I affect him, one way or another. "But I should… apologize, I mean."

His confession unsettles me. "What?"

"To your friend. I was drunk and I—"

Apparently, we really need to talk. Yet, if I'm being honest, that's not the reason that I led him here. Seeing him again is too good to be true. I have to push my luck. After all, he hasn't snubbed me yet. This mere fact bolsters my confidence. Cocksure, I take another step forward, entering his personal space this time. He lets me.

There.

My brain short-circuits, and I replay the scene from Paris, sliding my hand to palm his toned butt without requesting permission. The major difference is that, today, he's fully aware of what's going on between us and not complaining regardless. Quite the opposite, actually. My heartbeat thumps at a concerning pace, then all the blood in my body floods south. My semi turns into a full-on stiffy. His jeans are a useless barrier to my irrepressible need for him. He lets me.

Dazed, he gawks, his labored breathing slowly driving me insane. At last, his body goes lax, and he unfolds his arms. A smug smile forms on my burning face as my depraved mind interprets this action as surrender, and I immediately wonder whether he's going to kiss me.

In a bold move, I give his ass a firm squeeze. Lust ignites every inch of my skin as his half-mast eyes narrow. "I know you liked it then, just like you do now."

Don't you?

Once again, I keep my question to myself. The more this impromptu reunion inflames me, the more his body language changes. From immobile to stiff. From compliant to distant. From acceptance to denial. His brows knit, and he retreats until his back hits the wall. I hiss when my hand that's still firmly planted on his ass strikes the wall; that doesn't deter me, and I keep it in place.

"Get your fucking hand off me!" His command is delivered in an angry whisper, bordering on a plea. If he had expressed it earlier, I might have taken it seriously. His entire body melted like putty in my hands moments ago, and his eyes speak volumes. In any case, his next word contradicts both his tone and order. A strangled, even lower, "please" leaves his delectable mouth that I long to kiss again. Somehow, I release him from my hold, distressed, and provide the requested distance. No matter how willing he was to follow me, while visibly debating the idea, his potent presence overwhelms me. Backing down from my initial objective is beyond my control.

Must be why I'm just noticing his tight fists. The next thing I know, the jackass's fist forcefully slams into my stubbled jaw. No time to protest. No time to stop him. No time…

Fuck, that hurt!

The irony of the situation isn't lost on me as my knees wobble; I fantasized about doing the exact same thing the first time we met, and now, it's happening to *me*!

Groaning my disapproval, I rub my jaw, oblivious to the girl screeching behind me because I bumped into her while working to regain my balance and composure. My hunter instinct recovers, and I promptly assess the situation. As private as I'd wish to keep our reunion, I belatedly register that his knee-jerk reaction created a small gathering.

"Sorry about that, miss." I offer her my most candid smile, and she hands me a Sharpie to sign her collarbone. Why not, right?

I inwardly scold myself for my carelessness, driven by my testosterone rather than my rational brain. I'm hoping that nobody had the bright idea to film this; I wouldn't enjoy reliving it on social media. It's a little too late to worry about that. I didn't have time to think but should probably do some damage control. Dammit!

I turn their way, wink, and declare jokingly, "Guys, it's

okay." It's a business trip, and I'm here as a VIP; I can't damage my reputation or Nicolas's. "I'm Tyler Durden!"

That earns me a chuckle from the few who pick up on the reference. One of them starts, "The first rule of fight club is..." and trails off as the rest chant the remainder of the sentence. We continue in unison until we're at the third rule. Once we're done, I gently dismiss the prying eyes, informing them that I'll be back on stage shortly.

Meanwhile, Channing is frozen in place. His expressive green eyes are back on me, but I make sure the other patrons are back to minding their own business before I focus back on him.

We lock eyes, and I let him stew up to three Mississippi, then readjust my hat as I burst out laughing. "I probably deserved it." I wink, caressing the spot where he hit me. Because I'm a tease, I wet my lips to make sure that he's still with me. He doesn't disappoint, although he remains tight-lipped. "Now, be honest. You must've enjoyed it more than you care to admit. You've kept everything bottled up since we met that first time, didn't you?"

"Fuck you, Hunter," he warns in a deeper voice. Hearing him say my name sends sparks down my spine.

As much as I'd like to take him up on his offer, I refrain, knowing that I've toyed with him enough. Instead, I lean into his personal space again, my lips grazing his earlobe. "We're not done here."

His muscular body trembles, but I bet it's not due to fear. I give him some space. Antsy, he examines our surroundings, as if to confirm that we don't have an audience. "Go to Hell, cowboy." Once again, his words contradict his facial expression. Fire flashes through his eyes at the last word.

When I nearly suggest that he save a horse, I know that's my cue to go back to DJing. Turning away from him to do exactly that, he snatches my wrist and spins me back to where I was standing seconds ago. My hat falls and I don't care enough to grab it, but he does and replaces it without a word. His navy blue

T-shirt stretches with the effort of his inhalations. His hand wrapped around my wrist fascinates him as much as it does me. It feels like *déjà vu*. We look up at the same time.

The air between us thickens.

And just like that, my heart skips a beat when, with his eyes closed, Channing does the one thing I wasn't expecting.

Caves.

CHAPTER 8
APOCALYPSE

Mike

With my heart in my throat, I shut my eyes, cup his cheeks in my hands, and before I know it, my lips latch onto the cowboy's. I want to know. I need to know. I need *him* to know. Punching Hunter was liberating, but not as gratifying as expected, so I had to try another strategy to rectify the situation. This is my one chance to get even with him and get him out of my system.

The world around us vanishes the second his eyes meet mine. The noisy techno. The shouting voices. The evening chill.

Observing him shamelessly play tonsil hockey with *a woman* troubled me. What's his deal? I can't allow him to have it his way. Otherwise, what would that make me? Weak? This is my chance. He's at my mercy and has to pay for the humiliation that he inflicted at the club. For the little obsession his stupid hat became, haunting my days and nights. For the manhandling he dished in front of meaningless so-called new friends, but still.

His fucking hat doesn't get in the way; he must have cocked

his head to accommodate my awkward and demanding kiss. The more he pants, the more my face tickles as he willingly opens for me. There.

This is my call. I'm in charge here! I'll use the bastard's own tricks against him.

My tongue sweeps into his greedy mouth, and his shoulders instantly relax under my touch. I would have preferred some resistance rather than his soft chortle. One of my hands fists Hunter's fitted T-shirt and tugs him closer, my body going lax as I get reacquainted with his taste. Mint. Caramel. Male. My mind is set on its goal, but my traitorous body joins the party. A flood of conflicting signals ensues.

Focus, Clayton. This is payback. This is revenge. This is power.

The fucker chooses that very moment to press his palms against my chest and wrench us apart. My eyes shoot daggers; *I* was supposed to break the kiss!

"You don't get to decide when…" He trails off and smirks at me, his hot breath fanning over my crimson face.

"Fuck you, Hunter!" I snarl.

His hands linger on my chest a minute longer, branding me, then releasing me from his hold. "Be my guest." His deep voice is edged with filthy promises. Undressing me with his gaze, he readjusts his hat.

Grunting, I mentally berate myself for my poor choice of words. It's impossible to think straight when he's this close. As annoying as he is, I can't let him escape my clutches.

Out of reflex, my palms land on his taut chest and shove him out of my personal space. I need oxygen, and his presence isn't helping. Too bad he doesn't budge, his daring eyes capturing mine. "You and your…" I stutter and, before he says something inappropriate, quickly add, "big mouth."

A moan leaves his smart mouth. Seriously? "You know what

they say…" He shrugs, an amused expression on his conceited face. "Big mouth, big—"

Narrowing my eyes, I can't help but want to muzzle his smart mouth and put it to better use. He's impossible! Who says things like that?

The fucker unsettles me yet again by shooting me a raunchy once-over, licking his sinful lips. "Stop looking at me like that," I hiss.

What the hell does he want from me? We're not quite touching. His pupils are so dilated that it's clear, even in the waning sunlight. "Or what?"

Cutting off any chance of response, his commanding lips mold with mine and his arms circle my waist. I can't move. Once again, his lips on mine feel so wrong and, at the same time, so right. The friction of his stubble on my clean-shaven skin and the dance of his frenzied tongue with my greedy one send me into overdrive.

Whimpering, I wiggle as if possessed. Going a mile a minute, my brain is at war with my body, which craves more unprecedented sensations. The sloppy Parisian kiss the cowboy stole months ago enticed a hidden desire that has no place in my well-planned life. Worse, our encounter elicited sensations that I've been desperate to recreate in a flurry of one-night stands, but nothing's worked so far.

What's left of my willpower eventually propels me to stop the mind-boggling tongue action. He needs to accept that I run the show.

The air thickens between us as we huff and puff.

His half-mast eyes are so much darker than they were a minute ago. Should I keep playing with him?

"What'd you do that for?"

"You're not gonna win at this game, cowboy," I sneer in a rushed voice; an expression of my false bravado.

"So you think." Acutely attuned to my hungry body, one of Hunter's legs subtly treads closer and he leans into me.

Within seconds, his tongue fills my mouth again. Shuddering under his touch, my resolve crumbles as the asshat deepens the kiss. I stiffen when it evolves from bruising to tender, although our encounter is anything but. My body temperature skyrockets, along with my libido.

Unaware of the all-consuming passion that this kiss provokes in me, he thrusts his hip against mine, banging my back into the wall. His jean-clad semi rubs, grazes, and expands against mine that's desperate for release. I try to pace myself, but it's a lost cause.

Overwhelmed by a myriad of toe-curling sensations, my brain shuts down and allows my ravenous body to do the talking; maybe that's the kind of talking Hunter was referring to earlier!

Talk, my ass! No, no, no, keep my ass out of this!

With that thought in mind, my tempted body is given the green light to act.

Without warning, I close the gap between us and my knuckles trace his sculpted abs. At once, his intoxicating scent numbs my consciousness, and I act on the unthinkable the second his hands snake around my body. And just when I think the fever has reached its peak, the conniving man betrays me, ditching my waist in favor of my hair.

Why can't you stop? Get a hold of yourself. This is your game, not his…

Then why does the simple act of his fingers running through my short hair increase the unbearable pressure building between my legs? I don't even give a flying fuck if I come in my pants.

Damn, it's hot in here!

His urgent mouth devours my expletives and beads of sweat run down the side of my face, but I'm too far gone to swipe them away. I'm too blissed out to care. I'm too needy to break the spell quite yet. My senses are on alert. I want to hate him. I hate to want him. So much…

"More." His command that matches my thoughts is delivered between sexy little noises that should be kept in the bedroom, not expressed in a barely hidden corner.

I ache to yank him closer to force him to surrender before I do. My hand skirts north and settles on his neck. Apparently, any coherent thought telling me to get a hold of myself has vacated my mind. Drowning in lust, I lose track of time. I lose common sense. I lose myself in this heady kiss.

Once again, I heave a frustrated growl when he betrays me by abruptly breaking the kiss on his own terms. Panting, I come up for air. Sexed-up. I grumble my disapproval. Hornier. I growl my yearning. Disappointed. I grunt my frustration. My pulse trips over itself.

His limbs entangled with mine, he leans in closer, his uneven breath tickling my earlobe. "Open your eyes." Hunter's tone is firm, but soft. "Now!"

His harsh delivery flings me back to reality. I stifle a pained sigh, ignoring the opera ringtone associated with Matteo. I can't obey.

"Fuck you!"

"Interesting choice of words… yet again." His voice is collected, although my closed eyes heighten my senses, and I don't miss the sultry undertone.

Clueless to my runaway thoughts, he's acutely aware of my carnal desire. He continues to tousle my hair. I hate that he, of all people, is able to establish it as an erogenous zone. My body burns, yet forgetting my jacket wasn't the brightest idea. I'm assaulted by shivers that work their way down my aroused body.

Hunter repeats his command with a hint of irritation, and I freeze. This time, goosebumps appear for the wrong reason. This is wrong. This is so fucking wrong. He rests his palms on either side of my face. "Look at me, dammit, Channing!"

You know what, fucker? You don't deserve to know my name.
I'm going to win this game anyway.

Somehow, I'm forced to comply. It takes a second for my vision to adjust and settle on his talented mouth. "It's *me* you've been kissing." His thumb strokes my cheek; I'm on fire. "It's *me* you've been grinding against." The intimate gesture melts me. "It's *me* you've been longing for ever since our lips first touched." A dull ache forms in my gut. "Own up to it." The world spins, and I'm left weak, exhausted, and strangely alive.

What have I done?

I blink a couple of times to get reacquainted with the outside world, taking Hunter in. My raw urge for him needs to be tamed ASAP since I refuse to act on it again.

I'm not gay or bi or whatever. There's nothing wrong with that, but it's not who I am. I was teaching him a lesson.

Coughing into my elbow, I shake my legs to restart blood flow, but he blocks the way. The back of my neck hurts. He can't win. In a feeble attempt to escape, I whisper, "I need to go."

What have I done?

I pull my phone from my front pocket and shoot Matteo a quick text to evade eye contact. Of course, I lie and tell him that I left and am in bed with a headache, when I'm in the arms of a man with a boner.

What have I done?

"No, you don't." I don't miss his icy inflection, but his thumb travels to my swollen lips, making me lose focus as he untangles his body from mine without breaking visual contact.

"Fuck you!" I warn, regretting the words as they leave my mouth. I can't stand this toxic man.

I need to go.

"Just so you know, you owe me three fucks." His darkened eyes are filled with hunger. "Your call." He winks but lets out a bitter laugh, as if digesting that his fantasy won't become a reality.

Take that, dumbass!

"You don't need to go," the relentless man whispers to himself. Then, he startles me by sliding the tip of his tongue between my lips for one last quick kiss. I don't have time to process it before he turns away without peering over his shoulder, killing me softly.

"I do."

CHAPTER 9

THROUGH MY RAY-BANS

Troy

" I swear to God I'm not making this up," I roar, inadvertently attracting the attention of the other patrons surrounding the pool. The chubby redhead who's had her nose in a book for hours tilts her head my way. I watch her squirm in her chaise lounge through my aviator Ray-Ban sunglasses, and her own sunglasses slide down her nose. I offer a silent apology, and she returns her attention to her e-reader.

Up until a minute ago, I was in a semi-comatose state, lulled by the ocean on my day off... until Anna's name flashed on the screen and her excited voice replaced the music blasting through my wireless earbuds.

We've been at sea since leaving the Canary Islands three days ago. Soon, we'll be arriving in Maceio, Brazil, our last stop before disembarking in Rio. My patience is running thin; aside from France, I've never been outside of the US, and I can't wait to conquer the world! Did I mention that I'm having a blast performing here? I enjoy DJing, but this opportunity is beyond belief. Nicolas booked me a suite with a balcony; my gigs have gotten great feedback, and I feel like a rock star. Also, based on our most recent business talk, a record deal is within arm's reach. Needless to say, things are pretty good right now. My gut tells me that this day can't get any better.

"And, of course, you were minding your own business when you suddenly tripped and ended up lip-locked with Channing." Yes, his nickname is official! Her words convey a clear visual that I cut short because my swim shorts can only conceal so much. "You're incorrigible!" Anna goes into hysterics, and I wish that I could see her face as I disclose *the* news that's long overdue. Not willingly, mind you. Her new beau is keeping her busy—which couldn't make me happier, but that's no reason for spoilers—and I teased her via voicemail until she called back. I miss my friend; we tried a video chat once, but the connection was spotty, so we switched to calls. I imagine her dark blue eyes brightening with mischief as I recount how small the world is. "Did he taste as good this time around?"

He did.

But I'll keep that to myself for now. Instead, I share the nitty-gritty of how round two started and he eventually initiated our kiss. Every detail but one: how my heart lurched at his tightly shut eyes. I don't voice my concern, pretending that his earlier behavior is to blame. "How can you be so carefree about a guy who behaved so poorly?" My clammy hand grabs the glass of Diet Dr. Pepper from the small table. With each sip, nostalgia worms its way into my soul; I should book a ticket to Texas! I swallow the lump in my throat, focusing on the caramel taste instead.

"Oh, come on, Troy. Get over it, already! He was hammered and you taught him a lesson. I don't get this guy, though. It sounds like he didn't fight you much this time either. Of course, appearances can be deceiving, but from what I saw, I think he's straight... Groping me and all. And he didn't strike me as the type of guy who'd secure a ticket on a cruise for single people."

"Because you know him so well…" I trail off, finding her certainty about a complete stranger unnerving.

Ignoring my snarky remark, she asks, "Unless he's attracted to you, why would he give you a second chance to manhandle him?"

Did I bully him? I freeze at that, and when my half-asleep brain registers the other part of her assumption, my pulse accelerates. My attraction to him overrules logic, and it makes my stomach queasy. *Who am I to him?* The lingering question's repeated like a broken record since I saw him last. Almost a week ago.

"What happened next?" Curiosity colors her soft voice.

I take a deep breath, stroking the top of my wayward dark hair and thinking that I should probably make an appointment at the barbershop. "Well, you tell me." Then, I shrug, ignoring the fact that this isn't a video call.

"Huh?" She sounds like I knocked the wind out of her. My heart swells at how invested she is in my story.

"The guy vanished from the ship," I joke, fumbling with my phone to raise the volume.

"It's a giant ship. You can't run into him all the time!"

"Or he's avoiding me?" At the prospect of that, a crease forms between my brows. "Or maybe it was payback and he doesn't give a flying fuck about me." The unpleasant assumption hits me like a ton of bricks, and my throat constricts.

Can't be. I felt him melt into my embrace.

"Holy shit!" My hand tightens around the phone, and I bolt out of my lounge chair and snatch my T-shirt and towel, knocking over my Dr. Pepper in the process. My eyes pop out of their sockets and my mouth forms an O as the liquid splashes my quiet neighbor. "God dammit!" I berate myself aloud, instantly relieved that the cup won't cause too much damage since it's made of plastic.

With my hands full, I'm about to use my towel to wipe the

excess off of her sunburnt body. Her shades are off. Her eyes are glaring. Her breathing is exasperated. She vehemently shakes her head and steals the towel from me while I repeat my apology—for my cursing, clumsiness, and sheer stupidity. *My people skills suck.* Picking up the empty cup, I plunk it on the table and get back to my friend who's bombarding me with questions. "Listen, I'll have to call you back," I stammer.

"Wait, what's—"

I cut her off, although proper sentences are a challenge. "How can... he... I." I growl, zooming in on my prey. "I'm so fucking blind!" My throat is parched and my voice comes out raspy. I sigh; I owe her an explanation, right? "Speak of the devil... I just spotted him... on the other side of the pool. I'll call you back."

"Run Forrest..." Ha-ha! "Oops, figure of speech. Watch your step is more like it! Go hunt, big boy." She ends the call and my playlist resumes.

I hate that she's right. Hunter's back, full-throttle, but what's the point in sprinting around the pool, apart from making a fool of myself?

Pace yourself, moron.

I increase the volume to calm my frayed nerves and assess the situation. Grinning at my good fortune, I take him in. My shoulders loosen when I register the irony of the new song: Eric Church spying *Through My Ray-Bans... Sounds like me!*

My eyes follow him from afar. My mouth waters at the sight of him. My fingers itch to touch his impressive physique. Absentmindedly, I lick my lips, gathering my thoughts as I make my way towards him.

Am I ridiculous to chase after him when I was the one to ditch him both times?

My heart tightens. What do I have to lose? Worse comes to worst, he'll send me packing and we'll both ignore each other for a few more days, then go our own separate ways. Yeah, not much of a difference! Despite the weather, I quiver at the mere thought of how needy the bastard makes me. In the blink of an eye, my manhood hardens.

Shut up, buddy! Behave... for the time being.

Dwelling on what to do next, my feet have a mind of their own once he wraps up his conversation with his friends and leaves the premises. Like a moth to a flame, I'm overwhelmed by the pull that dwarfs common sense whenever he's near.

And guess what? Like the creeper I am, I follow him while keeping a reasonable distance.

I really am all over the place!

As usual, I inhale deeply and eventually tame my unruly emotions. Reaching my arms over my head, I manage to slip into my T-shirt while awkwardly carrying my stuff and following him to the lowest deck, which basically resembles the Wonderland Maze. This ship is massive, full of twists, turns, themed restaurants, and entertainment venues at every corner—besides strip clubs—and so many decks.

Shortly after, he pauses and I wait at the corner of a narrower hallway to the right. A couple of doors from where I stand, he swipes his keycard, hand on the handle, about to open the door. A pang of disappointment washes over me, and I berate myself. I'm such a fucking coward!

And when I think he's about to disappear into his cabin, he startles me by whirling in my direction. Thankfully, as he searches my eyes, he can't read anything since they're hidden behind my shades; his are tucked in the collar of his T-shirt. Soon enough, I'm torn from my reverie by his velvety voice.

"Stalker much?" A roar of laughter rattles the chest that I yearn to touch. As if bewitched, I stay there, breathless and unsure what I'm after. He scratches his solar plexus, where my fist touched him days ago. I stiffen. Is he doing this on purpose? "You could at least take off your glasses so..." He pauses. "I don't know..." He clears his throat. "Take them off. Please."

There's that word again. The same word. The same tone. The same despair. Odd, but I comply while striding his way.

Inhaling deeply, I brace myself, then exhale. "Listen, I think we started off on the wrong foot. I... We..." Am I at a loss for words again? This has got to stop! "Let me buy you a drink and settle our differences, okay? What do you say?"

"I'd say that you're a cheap dat—" His cheeks turn rosy as he stops in his tracks, grasping what he was about to say.

I shake off my annoyance at being called cheap, in favor of witnessing the embarrassment written all over his gorgeous face. The need to rescue him from his misery is stronger. It's time to let him off the hook and stop toying with his mind. After all, Anna might be right; if he's straight and drawn to me none- theless, he must be even more distraught than I am. Knowing where we stand will do us some good either way.

"Chill out, man. I'm not asking you on a *date!*" I hate the word and everything it entails, but that's none of his business. Heart hammering, I air quote the word and wink at the jackass, maintaining an even voice and some much needed distance between us... too afraid to maul him if I don't. "It's an olive branch, preferably involving alcohol."

To which, he winks. "Lead the way." It sounds more like a question, but I keep my opinion to myself.

Rubbing the back of my neck while following his suggestion, I worry my lower lip. "You sure?"

To say that I'm rattled by the implications hidden in his simple answer is the understatement of the year.

"Positive."

CHAPTER 10
RELAX

Mike

"So, you decide." Hunter's warm voice is expectant. "This or that?" He points his chin at either side of a crowded hallway where several themed eateries await.

"I'm tempted by the Happy Days diner." I shrug. "I like American classics! It'll bring back memories of the reruns I watched as a kid. I'm thinking that the sports bar will be noisier... and we're not here to watch a flat screen." I purse my lips. What I'm not telling him is that it exudes testosterone, and I doubt I'd be comfortable, considering the situation. "Am I right?"

My question is rhetorical, but he replies anyway, "Let's do *that*, then," stressing the word, his gaze playful, though I'm not sure why. Too bad... Damn, I have so many more questions for Hunter, but only so much that I'll allow myself to say out loud.

All in due time, Clayton.

Before I know it, his hand latches onto my elbow. Without another word, he sets us in motion, like he did the other night. Sure enough, this mundane gesture sends warmth across my skin. My sharp intake of air doesn't help matters. The effect this guy has on me makes no sense. Because, come on! He's a dude. I'm attracted to women. It seems that my confused cock didn't get the memo.

And let's not forget that you had his tongue down your throat... twice! The little devil on my shoulder might have a point. Hiding my inner conflict, I settle behind my poker face once we're seated in a booth that'll afford some privacy and order drinks. *Yeah, I got that, annoying devil.* I will myself to shut down that train of thought, schooling my features to hide my state of disarray.

"Aren't you expecting Fonzie to pop in? I know I am." His voice is light.

We discuss the atmosphere of the diner that's an exact replica of the one from the TV series and what brought us on this cruise. He erupts into side-splitting laughter when I explain how my best friend trapped me and eventually confess that it's not as bad as I'd anticipated.

Maybe his presence enhanced the appeal. Our first encounter remained a blur of anger and lust. At least seeing him again gave me the occasion to set things straight.

Actually, if anything, our last encounter proved that things are far from straight between us. Beyond my control, I let out a strangled noise.

"Everything okay?" Hunter's upper body leans across the table, his hand covering mine for a split second. Unless I dreamt it…

What the fuck is wrong with me?

"Yeah, sorry! I forgot something." I bite the corner of my lower lip, making up a story about my arcade plans with my friends that he doesn't know I already canceled in favor of feeding my curiosity.

Yeah, apparently I keep forgetting that I'm straight when you're around.

Given the size of the ship, I didn't expect to run into him

again. Declining his offer would have proven that I wasn't cool with getting a drink with *him*, that he means more than he actually does. No way, Jose!

I figured that my friends would pick apart my lame excuse; they didn't. So, postponing the peace offering by an hour didn't matter much. Although a few patrons appear to have wandered straight from the pool for an early dinner, we agreed that swim shorts and T-shirts wouldn't do. I pat myself on the back for suggesting that we change. Thank goodness his khakis and long sleeves conceal things that I shouldn't have noticed. Granted, each time that I bat my lashes, my eyes close a second too long and disturbing flashbacks assault my vision. How his biceps bulged when holding the girl the other night. How his shoulders seem broader than the last time we were in the same room. How his pants hug his ass.

Fuck! It's not supposed to be this way.

The reprieve doesn't seem as effective as I'd hoped. I welcomed a cold shower to dampen my horniness; that is, when paired with jacking off to the female porn star that I watched as soon as I locked the door. I replayed the images of how vocally she expressed her enjoyment. But my body was in knots and it took me forever to find my release, which isn't like me.

The buzz brought on by my second beer is slowly setting in, and I finally relax; that's all I need, whether it pleases my inner demon or not. I need to control my intake. He and I have already been down this road.

With that in mind, the conversation flows easily, and we talk about this and that. I don't miss how his gaze lingers on my face, though. When he's done with his Bloody Mary, we peruse the menu for dinner options. I don't miss how pained my breathing is. When the waiter delivers our burgers to the table, we rudely ignore him. I don't miss how our backs are glued to the booth. When the food reaches our mouths, we're fascinated. As much as we want to keep this casual, our body language tells another story.

But I carry on with the pretense because I'm genuinely interested in the enigma that he represents, in more ways than one. "I had no clue you and Monster Hunter were the same person!" I begin in between bites. Mmm... what a burger! "My friend, Matteo, is a huge fan. He dragged us to your gig..."

His face falls for a second before the lips that I long to taste again curve upwards. His ketchup-covered fries stop their journey in mid-air. "I take it you're not a fan." He wolfs them down, then what's left of his food. Damn, I can be such an insensitive prick!

Why would he need reassurance? His attitude reeks of self-confidence. Either I'm imagining things or I'm oddly in sync with him. Firmly believing that it's the latter, I try to make amends so he knows that it has nothing to do with him. "To be honest, electro isn't really my favorite. I'm more of a classics kinda guy... From what I heard, yours is—"

"Don't bother sugarcoating..." He chuckles. "Not *you*, okay?" His chocolate eyes caging mine, he sips on his water. I'm at a loss until he adds, "Not my favorite frenemy!" We laugh in unison, ignoring the elephant in the room. "Like any kind of music, it's not for everyone. There are so many genres." Talking about his influences and how he got his start in the industry is safer. From my frown, he guesses that additional context is necessary since I don't know the first thing about his idols. "Most of all, I'm into deep house." Eyes on his empty plate, he threads his long fingers through his dark hair while I drink him in, refusing to fight it this time. "Maybe it comes from my love of clubbing. I mean, I studied musical notation and performance but gave up playing cello after—" His cough is a feeble attempt to hide that there's more to his abrupt stop than he leads on. "Dancing's always been an escape, so mixing the music felt natural, you know?" I nod, thoughtful. "What about you?" His dark eyes seem to see right through me. Is he tormenting me on purpose, or is he utterly clueless?

With extreme difficulty, I calm my racing heart and manage to tell part of my story in an even voice. "My dark blue corporate lawyer suit needed hemming, so I pulled out my sewing kit, and three years later, I landed an internship as a fashion designer in Paris." I nurse my IPA, explaining the nausea that overwhelmed me when I stepped into my father's law practice each morning. I grimace at the mention of my dad but discard my sudden discomfort. "Sorry, TMI."

"No, no, no. No need to be sorry." He motions for me to carry on.

My breathing falters and I blurt out, "So, tell me. Bartending's your pastime in between gigs, is that it?"

"It is." I push my palms against the table to help me stand up. The world around me spins, and I'm well aware that alcohol isn't to blame. "Should we go?"

In truth, I'd rather stay where people forbid me from acting on my growing desire for a person that I'm not supposed to be attracted to. In truth, I'd rather stay in my overthinking head than envision my hands reacquainting themselves with his skin. In truth, I'd rather stay and pose all of the forbidden questions I have in mind. One prevails and entices my confusion...What's his sexual orientation?

I don't wait for his answer, and he follows me in silence. His nearness unsettles me as we saunter out of the restaurant, commenting on the food and the old jukebox. Ambling aimlessly, we walk side by side around the deck, and I begin rambling to appease my nerves. Why am I mentioning that I have a couple of vintage jukeboxes at home? Why is he grilling me on where home is? Why am I inquiring the same?

"So, we're practically neighbors!"

"I wouldn't say that Greenwich Village and Park Slope make

us neighbors. Close enough. It's a small world, though." He winks.

My erection comes to life yet again as I remember what followed the first time he said that.

Fuck, what are you doing to me?

Then it dawns on me that I'm talking, but he's gone radio silent. I search my surroundings, but he's nowhere to be found. He wouldn't have ditched me, right? A crease forms between my eyebrows as I turn around and find that he stopped at the previous intersection. My green eyes darken with worry… and pent-up desire.

When I join him, he asks, or rather commands, "Coffee. My cabin's down this way." He tilts his head, and I shiver, which must be all the approval he needs as he takes off at a sprint while fumbling with his iPhone that is soon placed in his pocket.

The door doesn't have time to close behind me before his mouth pummels mine.

So, amazingly good…

My back slams it shut when he rubs against me. The muffled sound resonates inside my head that's devoid of anything but the desire that this sexy individual instills in me. Only now do I hear the music in the background. An unmistakable song floats through a speaker that must be in his bedroom. *Whole Lotta Love* by Led Zeppelin. Such a sexy song. Such an obscene song. Such a classic song.

Scalding heat spreads across my skin as his masculine essence brands my brain, heart, and soul. No coherent thoughts are required. No further resistance is necessary. No more reasoning is useful. This kiss is rawer, yet softer than our previous ones because we both shaved. Why should I carry on with the comparison? My aroused mind chooses to make peace —for now at least—with the idea that I'm kissing a man for the third time… of my own accord. I smile against his mouth; it feels like a welcome home kiss, and I'm fine with it.

My entire being goes lax, and I let him angle my face to deepen the kiss. I'm at his mercy and that's okay. More than okay. Grabbing my butt. Grinding our lengths. Grazing my skin. His fingertips travel across my cheeks in fiery caresses but are soon redirected to pop open the buttons of my shirt, leaving goosebumps in their wake.

"Fucker!" I mumble, acknowledging his rough touch that's also oddly gentle. He chortles, nipping at my lower lip before trailing kisses along my collarbone. His TLC is both foreign and natural, making my heart sear. I grow more hooked on his scent with each breath. "More, Hunter." I don't recognize my own voice, and I writhe under his ministrations. Needier. My heart skips a beat. His kisses run down my chest while two fingers pinch my nipples. Hornier. My eyes enjoy the view. His hand slides inside of my pants and fondles my insanely hard boner through my boxer briefs. Dirtier. My avid mouth waters. His fingers make quick work of my button and fly and now easily stroke my greedy manhood with resolve.

This is the sweetest torture ever, and it still isn't enough.

"Please…"

CHAPTER 11
HOW BAD DO YOU WANT IT

Troy

His sexy plea stokes my fire. His mixed signals have vanished. His blatant desire doesn't leave room for doubt… but he has to voice exactly what he wants.

"I love how you react to my touch." My voice is no more than a strangled whisper, and I'm not even addressing him, but myself. The tip of my tongue traces a path along the hot skin of his neck. He fidgets against me while I teasingly stroke him over the fabric so he won't freak out.

His moans make my blood pound as his slightly hairy chest heaves up and down; his hair is so fair and sparse that I have to caress his skin to feel it.

"Then touch me more… I want more, Hunter." His fingers feverishly run under my dress shirt and explore my waist. The tickling sensation grows stronger, but I will myself to behave and focus on the task at hand.

I'm tempted to tell him my first name and request his, but now is not the time. "Explain."

"Stop teasing!" he groans. "Isn't it obvious that I want you?"

"You want me how? Tell me," I say in a rushed breath. The anticipation is killing me, making my heart thump in my chest and my stiffy throb against my zipper.

"You always this demanding?" His irritation and ardor speak right to my dick. With his question, his hand snatches mine and guides it into his boxer briefs, steering me so that there's no interruption between my strokes. "This… I want *this*."

My fingers circle his massive girth, my thumb caressing the tip of his impressive hard-on and smoothing the beads of precum that I find along his slit.

"Oh, fuck me!" he grunts, but his entire body freezes for a split second; he must be wondering if I'll take his exclamation as an invitation.

"Spell it out so there's no misunderstanding, baby." *Did I just call him baby?* Wow, I didn't see that one coming! But then again, I have his length in my hand, so it's not like he's a complete stranger, and calling him "man" felt more friendly than horny. "This?" I squeeze him harder. "As in my hand where it is now." He hisses, then growls and quivers. "Or that?" My tongue traces his earlobe. He gasps when I add, "As in my tongue on your cock." Subtlety has no business here. He has to decide what he wants. "Just so you know, I'll enjoy both. What about you?" I ask, deepening my voice. "So, which is it?" My favorite game is more fitting than ever. "This or that?"

"That… I want *that*… I want you…" He pauses to muster the courage to say, "I want your tongue on my cock." His heart races. "I… Suck me off… please."

There's that word again. My heart melts a bit more at his jumble of polite manners and crude words, while my free hand splays on his back and slides down to shuck his boxer briefs and pants in one swift move.

By the time his clothing lands at his ankles, my knees have already hit the plush carpet. His proud hard-on springs free.

Sweet! My tongue travels across my lips, anticipating his

taste. With a hooded gaze, I glance up. Our eyes lock and an indistinct emotion flashes across his face. Desire prevails.

"My pleasure." Without further ado, my hand that never stopped pumping him increases its speed.

His eyes are transfixed. His breathing is vocal. His face is flushed.

Happiness ripples through me as I let my tongue wander leisurely around his tip, swirling, getting acquainted with him. My other hand keeps busy fondling his balls; his gorgeous ass swings back and forth against the door like a pendulum.

Such a glorious sight.

Still rubbing his tip with my thumb, I gulp one of his balls into my mouth and massage it playfully with my tongue, then do the same to the other. Short breaths. Happy grunts. Erotic noises. I set him free. "Damn, I've wanted to suck your dick for so long," I profess between licks. It makes him smirk. Wait, wait, wait… That's not the reaction I'm after, although it does boost my morale.

Consequently, my daring stare hardens as I take all of him and he hits the back of my throat.

"Holy shit!"

Yeah, that's it!

His green eyes darken with need and don't falter as he pulls on my hair; I'm glad he chooses to keep his eyes open, otherwise I'd complain. Naturally, tonight's dinner conversation didn't include sexual preference; I have no clue what his experience with men is. What I've witnessed so far tells me that he's into me, and that's all that matters for now.

"Ohhhh…. Fuck…. I… You… Mmm… There…"

His fist grips my dark hair tighter, directing and imposing a rhythm as I take care of his ballsack and make a point of maintaining eye contact. I let him fuck my mouth, his grunts and expletives apprising me of his progress. As for my gag reflex, I'm confident that his widening eyes express both his surprise and pleasure. A smile tugs at the corner of my lips with the sound of his appreciation.

His hold loosens and, before I realize it, he runs his fingers through my hair. It makes me lose it for a reason that I don't quite comprehend. The sweeter he becomes, the faster I work him.

"You should... I'm... I'm gonna..." His hand on my head abruptly stops. His knees buckle with the building pressure. His lazy eyes laced with hunger express concern as he tries to warm me. My left hand claws his upper thigh to show him that I'm not going anywhere until I finish the job; the blowjob, that is.

Polishing off the evidence of his intense pleasure, I run my tongue over my glistening lips. I burst out laughing when his legs give way and he slides down on his bare ass as I get up. I'm fully-clothed. Fully satisfied. Fully erect. He stares at the bulge that tents my jeans. Leaning towards me, his hand covers it, which makes him shudder. He doesn't squeeze. He doesn't tease. He doesn't caress. Somehow, I find his unexpected boldness endearing, but that won't do because hesitation is written all over his face. It looks like he's getting acquainted with the idea. Too bad I'm too fucking horny to have a modicum of patience.

"Maybe it's best you don't start something you're not gonna finish." I bend his way to grab his hand and help him to stand. Relief washes over him, and he nods wordlessly, pulling his boxer briefs and pants back on in a brisk move. "Come on, I'll give you the grand tour." When he faces me, we realize that I didn't release my hold on his hand and we stay there, mesmerized. His gaze flits from our joined hands to my mouth, and he deposits what feels like a thank you kiss on it. I screw my eyes shut to bask in the gesture, then take him in. He wets his lips, which ignites my desire when I fathom that he tasted himself on my lips. He's hot as fuck. Plain and simple. "You really wanna make me cream my pants, don't you?"

"What are you? Twelve?" His tone is light, which reassures

me and instantly makes the weight on my shoulders disappear. "Jokes aside, I should sit down... I..." He trails off. *Guess I've drained him in more ways than one.* I grin at the thought. We amble to the couch of the humongous suite and sit down next to each other.

"I wasn't this gifted at twelve. Good thing I'm twice that now!" I wink, and then it hits me. "I'm Troy, by the way... Hunter's my last name."

"Mike." He offers me a goofy smile since we're still holding hands, tightens his grip, and shakes it. "Thanks for sucking me off, Troy. On another note, nice luxury cabin," he quips. It's clear that the grand tour was an excuse to get him to stay.

"Nice to meet you, Magic Mike. *De rien pour la pipe.*" I struggle with French, remembering Anna's classes. To my surprise, he winces at that. "My French pronunciation sucks that bad? It was supposed to mean: you're welcome for the BJ."

"Your French is fine and so is your accent. Sorry... I'm killing the mood. I shouldn't have reacted like that." His longer hair lessens the resemblance. "Being reminded of it constantly irks me sometimes, like people don't *see* me." He explains that the haircut was a prerequisite for Matteo's wedding.

Odd... Since when do weddings come with requirements?

"Trust me, I only have eyes for you, Mike. To be honest, the resemblance is closer to Big Dick Richie than Magic Mike."

Mike punches my bicep. "I can't believe you just said that!"

"What? Of course, I've seen the movie. Hot guys stripping, real acting, and an interesting story to boot... Right up my alley!" He jumps when I slap his upper thigh. "In case you haven't noticed, I was paying you a compliment. To make amends, let the cheap date treat you to a bottle from the mini-bar." I chuckle, then it dawns on me that I stupidly threw the word "date" into the conversation. Will he freak out like he did earlier?

His face reddens, but he quickly recovers. "Chill out! We're way past that. Good drinks in a relaxed atmosphere, delicious dinner with a fun guy, and an amazing blowjob on top of that. I'd say it's the best date I'd ever been on."

"I couldn't agree more." My foot taps on the carpeted floor. *Why am I nervous?*

"Now that I've recovered my senses, I want you to know that I meant it."

"Meant what?"

He coughs into the crook of his elbow. His gaze lowers to his feet, then his eyes bore into mine. "I want more... I... I've never been with a dude before." His cheeks are pink, but his lust-filled eyes strip me bare; his newfound determination speaks directly to my soul. "As much as I hated you at first... I... I felt something that scared the shit out of me. Now that I think about it, I can't allow fear to dictate my life, you know?" He pauses. "I want you."

"Wow, that must have been a hell of a blowjob!" I tease to lighten the suddenly serious mood, brushing the top of his hand that rests against the back of the sofa.

"You asshole." He tips my way in a feeble attempt to make me fall to the side that fails miserably. When we sit straighter, I notice that he's inched away from me. He shivers, an apologetic expression on his previously blissed-out face.

It takes me two seconds flat to get why. "Listen, it's late and your cabin is on the other side of the ship." My words have the opposite effect, and he tenses, so I scoot closer and slip my hand into his. "I'm sorry. That came out wrong." I bend towards him and give him the sweetest kiss I can manage, although all I want to do is ravage his impressive body. "I'm not asking you to leave. I'm asking you if you'd like to stay and spend the night." His face turns beet red. "I promise I'll behave. I can be a gentleman sometimes, you know."

"I'm not after a gentleman."

"Well, from my understanding, you aren't after a man..."

"*Touché.*"

"Look, I'm no shrink, but I'm more than willing and able to help you overcome your fears in that department. I think there shouldn't be any elephant in the room or forbidden words. Like asshole. Like straight. Like bi." I impart enough for him to get that I'm not a predator or trying to put a ring on him. "I truly like you, though. I think we have great chemistry that we should explore further. No need to freak out; I won't ever talk you into something that's a hard limit. We have a few days left on this ship." To coax him, I plant a quick kiss on his lips. "Let's see where it leads us and enjoy ourselves in the meantime. Extra toothbrush in the bathroom. Extra T-shirt in the drawer. Extra pillow in the closet." The vein on the side of my forehead throbs as my blood boils. "You are addictive. Your dick is addictive... Your ass is safe with me... unless you change your mind. There are boundaries that your upbringing, culture, and beliefs have forbidden you from testing. I respect that. Now is not the time for spoilers, but you might actually find pleasure in what I'm ready to offer you." The whole time, his eyes alternatively narrow and widen. I lit a fuse that he needs to be comfortable with. It's his call, as it was when he returned my first stolen kiss. "So, bed or door?"

"Bed."

CHAPTER 12
WALLS

Mike

Talk about a rude awakening! Emerging from my blissful slumber, I bolt out of bed, collect my scattered clothes, and put them on in haste. Troy's cabin reeks of sex, and I have no complaints there. "Troy, wake up!" Concern colors my voice, and I scold myself for my rudeness. No good morning. No morning kisses. No morning caresses. Right now, the evidence of my presence should be erased. Once I'm dressed, I take in his sleeping form for a second like the creeper I've become. His back's to me and he's curled up in the fetal position. Lost in my desire, I rub the back of my neck. Coming to my senses, I shake my head and lean across the massive bed to reach his shoulder, hidden under the fluffy comforter. "Baby, get up."

Yup, we're already on a term-of-endearment basis. Sue me!

I rock his taut body to speed the process. He tosses and turns, making several sexy noises that I've come to love in the six amazing days we've spent together. Six. Amazing. Days.

Days? Well, nights mostly. While he's busy DJing, I snuggle in his bed. Expectant. Horny. Curious. Needless to say, I steer clear of his gigs for numerous reasons; my dislike of electro isn't even the main one. Not being seen together ranks higher on the list; thank God for texts. Granted, quite a few patrons witnessed our reunion, but at least neither my friends nor his manager were privy to our make-out session. Our unexpected "date" wasn't broadcast either; I intend to keep it that way. Troy claims that his sexual preference shouldn't matter in the music industry, but being the one who jeopardizes his shot isn't an option.

We're not an item, we're a situation… and we simply can't get enough of each other. Hence, staying at his place remains a safer bet. Hence, entertaining my own friends happens while Troy sleeps or works. Hence, getting action primarily involves my boner and his mouth. And let me tell you, he's a man of many talents!

I wish I could reciprocate. Lying to my friends about an upset stomach as an excuse to stay in bed with him while everyone else left and explored Maceio had been my idea in the stupid hope that it would unlock what I refer to as my gay side. Well, it did, up to a point.

Believe it or not, my brain accepted our bare bodies. After the initial revenge kiss, the notion of initiating a kiss with a man, with *him*, took some time… but didn't feel foreign by the end of the day. Neither did caressing or licking his skin. I don't deserve the patience he exhibits when he repeats that it's okay to take it one step at a time and praises my determination. The inequity of the situation bothers me; he's made me come time and time again and then scurries off to take care of himself in the privacy of the shower so that I'm not uncomfortable. I regularly apologize for my cowardice. As much as I enjoy waking up in a tangle of limbs, his prick and our asses are forbidden zones, so we keep dry humping like teenagers.

With one knee on the edge of the bed, I kiss the hollow of his neck. "Someone's at the door." My whisper prompts a groan, muffled by the comforter. "Troy, come on!"

"Go get the door, then," he whines. His gruff voice only lasts for a couple of minutes after he regains consciousness in the morning, and it gets me hard every fucking time! Oblivious to my growing need, he shoots me a happy smile when he turns my way. Tossing the cover aside to expose his glorious nakedness, he pries one eye open. *Damn, he doesn't realize how sexy he is.* "And after that..." His eyes strip me bare.

I play dumb and don't give him the opportunity to finish, peppering sweet kisses on his neck and ignoring his goosebumps and semi. "You and I both know that I can't do that." My heart tightens. I'm his distraction. He's my experiment. We're each other's addiction... Shouting it from the rooftops would be stupid. Tonight, we'll part ways. I'll explore Brazil for a month. He mentioned the potential of returning to the States for his record deal. I doubt that the future holds anything more for us. Still, I can't let go.

The pounding at the door escalates. In less time that it takes to draw my next breath, he bolts out of bed stark naked, holds either side of my head in his splayed palms, and sweetly murmurs, "Stay put. Okay?" To conceal his impressive morning wood, he grabs a pair of sweatpants on the way.

I can't breathe. *What if the person insists on coming in?* My heart is about to explode. Sitting on the bed, I bite my nails while he apologizes to his manager for sleeping in and informs him that he'll join him for the business breakfast in fifteen. I hear the door closing, and he's back at my side in no time. Standing in front of me, he gazes at me, a wicked grin on his face, then drops to his knees. He palms my face before nibbling on my lips and rubbing my left shoulder. "You're awfully tense!" His deft fingers lower my zipper. "We're safe, baby. Let me get you off and have my appetizer."

I can't relax. "I should go." My heart tightens as I twirl his curls around my fingers and my other hand covers his to make him stop.

"That's your go-to line when you're pissed, huh?" Grumbling, he presses his hand on my solar plexus and pushes me.

"You know, sex isn't the answer to everything," I claim as my back hits the bed. My entire body grows cold, heart included.

Unfazed by my reluctance, he straddles me and his mouth conquers my mouth... my body... my better judgment.

I can't let him. "I should go... I... can't do this."

LET'S SEE... I completely screwed this one up, didn't I?

Beads of sweat run down my spine and collect at the small of my back, making me fidget on the beach towel. The masochist part of me is grateful for the discomfort brought forth by the abnormally hot May weather in Rio. This is what I deserve for acting like an asshole. Relieved to be lying on my stomach, I shamelessly enjoy the friction that stirs my manhood to life. I guess that's all the action it'll be getting for the balance of my vacation.

Stella's high-pitched voice tears me from my pity party. "Do you mind putting some lotion on my back?" I tilt my head in her direction. She bats her eyelashes and hands me the sunscreen. Without further ado, she plops onto her stomach, holding her long blonde hair to the side.

In order to be presentable in short order, my twisted mind sends me a flashback of the bar exam, my most unwelcome memory, way worse than my hospital stay. I had no desire to follow in my father's footsteps. The strategy works like a charm, and I comply absentmindedly, thinking of *The Girl from Ipanema* because that's who she is to me.

"You know, our cruise was so much fun..."

I tune her out and nod whenever she turns my way. Technically, she's not from Ipanema; that's where we are. Technically, she's not tall and tan; who cares if she doesn't look like the girl from the song? Even the stupidest guy on earth would pick up on her flirtatious nature when we met up with the bridal party two days ago in Rio. She'll be the maid of honor, and in a couple of days, I'll be standing next to her as Matteo's best man.

Thankful to be around my usual group of friends, I nonetheless get lost within my head in no time. No matter how surreal my interlude with Monster Troy seems now that I've escaped his spell, I can't deny it. Last night, the alcohol loosened the girls' tongues and each conceded that they'd kissed a girl in college. In between drunken giggles, they explained that it was a rite of passage and consequently kissed again, making the men hard. Every man but me. I want to believe that Troy was nothing but an experiment, but that's clearly a crock of bullshit. This man made my body come alive like no one else... and that means something.

Am I gay? I've checked out other good-looking guys since then; no spark. But I'm not immune to Stella's charms, simply perplexed.

Am I gay? Ever since I kissed Troy back in Paris, I kicked around the idea, especially when Lisa rubbed salt in the wound by reminding me that I couldn't get it up. The perk that arose from our failed one-night stand is a witty new friend... even better!

Am I gay? I never faked my attraction to women and have since proven that the Lisa incident was a one-time thing. However, my reaction to Troy has led me to question my sanity. Raw. Primal. Uncontrollable. And yet, I battled my desire for him.

I haven't texted Lisa since I boarded the cruise ship in Marseille, but I'm pretty sure that she would shit a brick if she could read my current thoughts!

Once Stella's body is thoroughly slathered with sunscreen, I get up, scrunching my nose at the sticky residue on my fingers.

"It's too hot. I'm going for a swim," I declare, knowing full well that she won't follow me until her sunscreen is absorbed.

Swimming will cool my boiling head and clean my sweaty body. She expresses her disappointment, but I offer to take her to dinner to brighten her gloomy mood; I need to put my post-Troy theory to the test and give her a try. Her signals are loud and clear. Taking her to bed won't even be a challenge.

Hours later, the plan unfolds as expected. Her red lips are wrapped around my shaft, but that's not how I want my release. Her luscious feminine curves also speak to my brain. Her long silky hair is securely fisted in my hand as I take her from behind moments later. Sliding into her inviting pussy feels both comforting and odd. Pounding into her is both satisfying and insufficient. Getting us off doesn't take as long as I'd hope, which is both shocking and disappointing. Considering we'll be in close quarters until we get back to the US, I suggest a repeat if we agree to my terms. No commitment. No relationship. No future. Since when have I become so shallow? I've always wanted to experience a deep and meaningful connection with someone. And look at me now, insisting upon non-committal sex!

It takes me a week to grow a pair and explore a side of me that Troy unleashed. Hooking up with Stella until we part ways in New York doesn't make sense anymore; at least, I'm honest with someone. It's time to do the same with myself.

Who would have thought that pay-per-view could help? Slightly inebriated to take the edge off, I'm naked in my lonely hotel bed. Soon enough, my breathing grows labored. I haven't watched porn in months; it's as efficient as ever. Soon enough, my skin's on fire. I can't fathom why witnessing other people fuck is so arousing. Soon enough, my erection is engorged. The close-ups are kind of too much. The dirty talking is too much. The humongous penises are way too much. But it does the trick. This time, though, I sit on my hand until I almost burst. With my heart thumping in my chest, my release is fast, messy, and powerful.

Fuck, that felt awesome!

Spent, I lean to the side of the bed to snatch some tissues from the box on the nightstand and clean up my sticky abs and hand. Resolve courses through me, and I grab my iPhone, scrolling through my contacts.

Mike: I shouldn't have skulked like I did.
You didn't deserve it. You've been nothing but nice.
I shouldn't have left the ship without saying goodbye.

Hope skyrockets when three little dots flash on the screen, indicating an incoming answer.

Troy: Goodbye.

What? That's all I get? Yeah, yeah, I fled like the coward that I am because the chance of someone—anyone—knowing that I allowed another man to touch me inappropriately suffocated me in a flash. Literally.

Mike: Let's get together. I'll explain.

Troy: Can't. It's a little too late for that.
Explain what anyway?

My heart lurches. I deserve to be brushed off, but I was hoping…

Mike: Can't or don't want to?

Troy: I'm back in NY. I intended to share
my plans with you, in case you were interested.
Clearly, you weren't and left me no choice.
Explain what?

Mike: What? Already?

> *Troy: Nothing tied me to Rio.*
> *Had a business meeting to attend.*
> *You vanished and went incommunicado, Mike.*
> *You're lucky I'm in a good mood today.*
> *Explain what?*

No emojis are paired with his texts as was previously the case. It's probably his way of keeping his distance... via text. I would prefer to tell him in person, but evidently, I don't have much of a choice.

Mike: I just watched porn.

> *Troy: Good for you!*
> *Is that what prompted this convo*
> *after you ghosted me for over a week?*

Mike: I guess.

> *Troy: Should I be proud or offended?*

Mike: I'm sorry, okay. That's what I want to explain.
I want to try. Us. Together. Please...

> *Troy: An epiphany, thanks to porn?*

Typing becomes excruciatingly difficult. He doesn't push me. Clearing my throat, I hate that it constricts as I type.

Gay porn.

CHAPTER 13
MADE FOR YOU

Troy

After immersing myself in the electro world, I need to recharge with country music. Blake Shelton's latest album, which I've been playing on repeat, is replaced by another familiar voice.

"Look, I'm about to board a plane to New York." Grabbing my carry-on, I join the already crowded boarding line in LAX. I make a point to keep my voice low since I'm talking through wireless earbuds. "What's all that racket on your end?"

"Woke up at the crack of dawn. I'm shooting a commercial today. Thought it'd be easier to reach you at this time of day. Don't worry, you're not on speaker!"

"Ha-ha." As if my sex life's a hot topic! "Nothing to report anyway."

"Really?" Her raspy morning voice is tinged with bewilderment.

"Unfortunately, yes. And this isn't the place."

"Yeah, I figured. Was just touching base to see how you were doing."

Good question, Anna! "The answer's pretty simple. Tired

from bouncing between LA, Miami, and Vegas for the last two weeks." Trust me, I'm far from complaining. Since stepping off of that cruise ship last month, things have spiraled in the best of ways. "Happy that my career's finally picking up now that I'm a signed artist." A rush of heat unfurls along the back of my neck, and I still can't wrap my head around it. My eyes lose focus with the next confession. "Confused by Mike's mixed messages." I disembarked the ship with a signed contract in one hand and a bag full of questions in the other.

What the hell happened between Mike and me? It's not my style to crawl back to someone like a lost puppy. It's not the first time that someone's rejected me. It's not like we exchanged vows or anything. I know better than to beg for an explanation. "Thing is, I truly like the guy." My admission makes me cough into my jacket-covered elbow; I hate that it's almost July, but I can't wear a T-shirt because of the blasting air conditioning! "What pissed me off, though, is that I thought we'd been honest with one another." I sigh as I remember how the jackass slipped through my fingers the day that the cruise ended. "So he went radio silent for a week, then texted me out of the blue and said we should meet."

"Well, put yourself in his shoes for a sec. You basically mauled him... twice!" I'm about to protest her allegations, but she carries on. "I'm perfectly aware that he returned the kiss... twice, thank you very much. I'm keeping tabs on you two. What I'm saying is that you guys have been playing cat and mouse since day one. Maybe he's trying to adjust to the idea, you know? He told you he's never been with a dude before." Anna's words ring true, but Mike's behavior when things got more intimate contradicts them.

"He didn't seem afraid, if you ask me... Eager would be more like it." I was about to say horny... No need to have people eavesdrop on our convo, which should be held privately. I can only handle so much of her Psych 101. "Whatever... I'll call you back later today. Okay?"

"Got it! All in all, I'm glad things are working out for you. I'm so proud of you, big boy!" She pauses. "As for Mike, give it some time."

"That's all I've been doing!" I complain, pursing my lips to contain the verbal diarrhea that threatens to bust loose. Fatigue increases my frustration, which, in turn, makes me ridiculously verbose. "Anyway, let's not get into that right now or I'll miss my plane." I search for my ID in my jacket pocket and take a couple of steps as the line inches forward.

"Sure. Text me when you're available. We'll find a way to make our schedules work... Maybe I should pay you a visit. I miss hugging you." Anna's definitely a tactile person.

"I miss you, too, Anna. Text and FaceTime have their limits. You know you're welcome to crash at my place, right? We could go to that new club in Manhattan. It's called Studio 45. It's as popular as its ancestor, Studio 54, but less disco, more electro, and a mixed audience." I know that she can read between the lines and determine that it's my hunting ground, primarily targeted at LGBTQ patrons, but straight people are also welcome. As my friends became aware of my sexual preferences over the years, I've learned not to discuss such topics in crowded places, such as airports; you never know who might be listening and is keen to grace you with their unsolicited opinion. "My place in Brooklyn is in a trendy neighborhood." My Park Slope apartment was the first investment that I made with my incoming cash flow. "The one thing, though, is that it just has one bedroom and I don't own a futon. Of course, I could sleep on the couch and let you and your beau stay in the bedroom, but just so you know, there's only one bathroom."

"That's a very American concern, my friend!" she retorts. "Apparently, you haven't lived in Europe long enough to grasp that it isn't such a big issue for us. Oh well, I'll try to land a contract for an American campaign. That'll give me the perfect excuse to come and see you... and talk about music, love, and sex! I'll talk to you later."

And with that prospect in mind, Anna ends the call without further notice and I board the red-eye. It isn't long until I crash from exhaustion, which offers a welcome reprieve. These past couple of days have been intense and so successful that Nicolas sounded even more thrilled than I was the last time we talked.

Breakfast on board isn't to my liking and neither are any of the flight attendants, so I refrain from harmlessly flirting with them to pass the time until we land. That's okay, though. It seems like I can't get my favorite frenemy out of my head anyway. After his confession about jacking off to gay porn, I've strangely been friend zoned; the nature of our texts has become mundane over the last few weeks. Our whereabouts. My music. His job hunt. I care about these things, but not to the point where these are the sole subjects that we can talk about. Maybe calling him or getting together once I'm back for a couple of days might help. So far, it's more frustrating than when we weren't talking at all. What was I saying about mixed signals?

The sliding doors open to the real world. Damn, I've missed New York! Granted, Newark isn't quite Manhattan, but it'll do; it's hardly past 7:00 a.m., so way too early to care... I'm so *not* a morning person!

Grumbling at my terrible idea of booking the red-eye, I find my suitcase on the carousel and head towards the exit. All the while, I remain unaware of my surroundings, with my head stuck in my iPhone searching for the Uber app to arrange a ride home.

I'm almost done with the reservation when I'm interrupted by a masculine voice that baffles me, warms my less-than-romantic heart, and makes my dick twitch. *Am I dreaming this because of my earlier call with Anna?* When I look up, reality dawns and my mouth hangs open in shock. And to think that I stored my hat in my luggage to be less conspicuous. What an epic failure!

"Good morning, cowboy!" the bastard slurs, winking at me as if his presence is the most natural thing on earth. His tone is more friendly than flirtatious, but seeing him in person makes my heart skip a beat. *Why does this guy affect me so much?* For all I know, apart from test-driving me, he's not that into me.

Facing him, I stand at arm's length and take him in. Brawny body. Dreamy eyes. Sinful mouth. Far enough to thwart his familiar scent from permeating my nostrils. Close enough to remember how he felt thrusting in my mouth, which instantly waters as I long to taste him again. Still, I can't help but blurt out the lingering question that burns my tongue. "What the fuck are you doing here?"

"Glad to see you, too, man."

I'm too shell-shocked to produce a witty reply. I guess my brain short-circuited at the sight of a smiling, unshaven, and hot-as-sin Mike. "What's with the hat anyway?" Mike's wearing a straw cowboy hat that's rather similar to mine!

"Don't tell me that you forgot my warning from my last text."

In a feeble attempt to recall what I said, I narrow my gaze on him, detailing his beautiful features instead of concentrating on our conversation.

He snaps his fingers to snap me out of it, and I mindlessly shake my head. "I'm listening." *What was he saying again?*

"I told you that next time I wouldn't look anything like Channing Tatum and you might not like it." Seeing his rosy cheeks under the hat that regrettably hides part of his gorgeous face is endearing. My heart swells that he's worried about what I might think. "My hair has grown, but not enough, so I thought you might enjoy my new accessory, considering how your cowboy hat haunted me!"

Mike: 1 – Troy: 0

My reaction to him annoys me, but why not speak my mind? "Haunted you, huh?" I tease. He's oddly at ease with our interaction in a crowded place, although it's beyond friendship. So I lean into his personal space and murmur into his ear, "You're sexy as fuck either way, and I like you way too much for my own good." I take a step back and am pleased that, for once, he proudly wears his emotions on his flaming face.

Well, I'm not going to make a scene in the airport, so I might as well go with the flow. He's here, isn't he? I didn't think that he'd pick up on the scattered hints regarding my arrival.

Mike: 2 – Troy: 0

"It looks good on you!" I eventually admit. My feet are glued to the floor, and I'm captivated by this man. "You know I don't wear mine outside gigs because I don't like to draw attention in the city that never sleeps."

"Well, I wanted to attract yours. You were too busy with your phone at first, but I could tell by your face that I succeeded anyway." He shrugs while worrying the corner of his lip. "So... I'm here because I thought that it would be nice for you to be greeted by a familiar face instead of an Uber driver... I happen to have a car, and I'm offering you a ride. That is, if you forgive me. Like I said, I was an asshole to you. I gave this a lot of thought, and I want to start over. Will you forgive me? Please..." With that, he takes two steps towards me, entering my personal space.

Mike: 3 – Troy: 0

"I want to give what we started a try... give it a try... give us a try." With that, the friend zone vanishes. I'm not going to call him out on his inconsistency, that's for sure. "I can't stop thinking about you." I pull short intakes of air to suppress the urge to kiss him right here. "Every goddamn minute." Impervious to my escalating yearning, Mike angles his face in such a way that his hot breath grazes my earlobe and speaks straight to my aching dick. "I've never wanted anything as much as I want you, Troy Hunter." Now, I'm thankful that my jacket conceals the evidence of my arousal. "So, which is it?"

"What do you mean?"

"This or that?" Oh, now he's playing *my* game. He leans closer and questions in a whisper, "I mean, would you rather have my lips wrapped around your cock or be balls-deep in my ass?"

What? Did he just mention my cock and his ass without stuttering? "You can't be serious! I didn't ask for that!" My throat constricts. "That's not fair, Mike. You're tempting me with options I'd enjoy, knowing full well that you're not going to follow through."

"Says who?"

CHAPTER 14
PIECE OF MY HEART

Mike

There's no awkward silence during the forty-minute drive to Greenwich Village. There's just two guys bringing each other up to date on what happened in LA or what triggered my unexpected departure from Rio. There's screaming when I open the door to my gigantic brownstone.

I noticed how Troy's brown eyes widened as he slid into the passenger seat of my brand spanking new BMW in the airport parking lot, but he didn't comment. After all, what's the big deal? It's not like I'm sixteen and bought my first car!

"How many of you live here?" His jacket slips from the crook of his elbow and falls to the floor as he turns in every direction in the middle of the foyer.

"What do you mean, how many? I already told you that I'm single. I'm too old to have roommates, so it's only me. Why?" It's odd how his questions rattle my nerves. *Am I pretending to be okay with having him here?* I shake my head absentmindedly, chasing the stupid thought away, and it's replaced by warmth settling low in my gut. My hand has a mind of its own and circles his wrist. We lock eyes. The heat turns to an irrepressible hunger for the person that I'm not supposed to be drawn to, but undeniably am. Touching him was a bad idea; it'll undoubtedly lead to swapping spit in the entryway, which isn't how I want this to go. Damn, my attraction to this guy is surreal.

"I don't understand. I thought all Manhattanites lived in apartments. This is more like a house." He breaks eye contact and adds in a whispered voice, "This is bigger than the house where I spent my childhood near Dallas, and there were seven of us."

Now he's the one who sounds odd. His voice. His words. His demeanor. It's the first time that he's revealed something personal, and from the way that his eyes focus anywhere but on me, I sense there's something there. Yeah, he rubs the back of his neck, so it's not the time to press the issue. Large family, but he didn't say that he *grew up* there… My pulse accelerates as my overthinking head worries that he might have lost his parents or something. It's not the time to pry quite yet, so I make a mental note for later…

Damn, I'm seriously considering a later *with a dude! What has he done to me?*

I disregard my apprehension and focus on the initial topic. "Yeah, it's pretty big, but I knew this four-floor apartment was mine from the second that I stepped inside! The basement's also fully finished," I brag, realizing that this piece of information might sound on the abductor side. Nah, it's perfectly normal to discuss my place's layout.

Relax, man!

My brows knit and I fumble with my phone to put some music on. The moron that I am snickers at the irony of the random song, although I don't want to apply pressure. *I'm Your Man* by Leonard Cohen. How fitting! I glance at him; his eyes convey mirth. He and I both know why we're here, right? Clearly, it's not to shoot an episode for HGTV. His eyes meet mine and his fingers reach for my hat, discarding it on the long black leather couch in the living room. His head swivels, and before I know it, his lips sweep across mine while his thumb rests behind my ear. The sweet gesture is so unexpected that it makes my entire body quiver in anticipation. I'm not nervous, merely expectant, but I need to buy myself some time. *Am I going to let him fuck me? For real?* I break the kiss and rub the back of my stiff neck, saying, "If you behave, I'll give you a quick tour. I know that it's bigger than the cabin, so the tour will take a bit longer. Let's go." For no other reason than to show him the way, my fingers crook and snatch his. My skin grows feverish. I can't wait to be naked with him again.

"Must be a hassle to clean such a huge place," he jokes when we arrive at the small backyard that's encased between the adjoining buildings' walls and designed to protect the area from prying eyes. It's not suffocating, rather a little slice of heaven in the madness of a busy city.

"Right. It's a good thing that I'm not stuck doing it myself then. Come on, you haven't seen anything yet."

A sly smile forms on his face. "Well, climbing the numerous stairs is a good workout." Of course, he's joking, considering how in shape he is. The second we arrive at the landing, he glances up and we both burst into laughter since this floor is mostly occupied by my private gym.

We stay on the threshold of the open-plan workout space. "See, it's like you read my mind. Climbing the stairs is the warm-up. I have some gym clothes if you feel like working out." His lower lip covers his upper one, and I cock my head towards the next flight of stairs. "Upstairs is the guest area, and the top floor is the master bedroom." I swat his ass to get him moving.

A sigh escapes my mouth as we both catch our breath.

"By the way, how did you know which flight I'd be on?"

Running my fingers through his hair, I stifle a grin. "It took you long enough to ask!"

"I… I guess I was too stunned by your presence. Then, I tried to make sense of it…"

"It may come as a surprise, but I pay attention. A couple of your texts hinted when you'd be back." I cough lightly. "Also, sometimes connections and money help."

"Sometimes?" His strangled voice comes out as a question.

"Yeah, let's leave it at that or you'll think I'm a stalker and that's how we ended up on the same cruise." I'm not revealing my sources. "Wanna grab a shower?" My cheeks burn at what my attempt to change the subject implies. "I mean, with the plane and everything… I thought that maybe… you…"

Within two strides, the man that's been front and center in my thoughts and dreams stands in front of me. Ohhh, so close! My breath hitches as his familiar scent returns, igniting my craving like none before him.

His heavy lidded eyes strip me bare while his thumb caresses my stubbled cheek.

Well, fuck me! Oops, figure of speech. Am I up to the challenge that I bragged about earlier? Maybe, maybe not. Not yet… I'm so screwed. Damned English language!

"I've missed you." His sensual lips tease my parted ones. "I've missed this." Next, the tip of his tongue traces the contours of my mouth. This gesture alone makes my cock throb, and I melt into him, getting reacquainted with us and splaying my hand on his gorgeous ass to bridge the unbearable distance between us. "I've missed us." He claims my mouth in the softest kiss that I've ever received. Unfortunately, he breaks it too soon, so I rub our semis together. "It's okay to be nervous, Mike." His breathing becomes ragged. I fucking love how I affect him. "The rules we established stand; let's take this one step at a time." His fingers wander to my hair. Scalding heat spreads across my skin. "If there's something you wanna try, let me know. I want to make this… journey good for you. I'd rather you voice it so there's no confusion."

"Thank you. I'm not afraid, you know…" I kiss him briefly. "But my bravery might have… limits. Honestly, I want it. I really do. It took some getting used to, but I'm over pretending that I'm solely into women." My breath seizes in my throat. "And you were right, by the way; gay porn was an epiphany. To be honest, I never imagined getting so turned on by watching guys fuck." I chuckle at my admission. "I mean, some of the first clips I found were pretty gross, which happens. Then, I unearthed what both of my heads enjoyed."

"Good! Let me know how I can make this a reality if that's what you want."

I mouth a silent thank you, my hungry eyes doing the rest of the talking. "I want this to be good for both of us. I'm concerned about my lack of experience—"

"Don't! One step at a time, remember?" He makes quick work of our buttons and zippers. Our pants fly, and our T-shirts are next. Standing there in boxer briefs doesn't faze me. I want more. My eyes flicker, and I notice things about Cowboy Troy that I normally wouldn't when looking at a dude. The way his enticing cologne mixes with his masculine scent and fills the room. The way his biceps flex in an appealing way that makes my tongue impatient to lick his skin. The way his full mouth is so well-defined that I can't wait to have it wrapped around my shaft again. I shouldn't be noticing that, but I do and I'm okay with it. "I'm right where I want to be with a man that I can't get enough of." His last words are strangled, and I kiss his temple, pleased that he's as overwhelmed as I am. "You mentioned a shower… Care to join me?" His brow arches.

Should I let him know that abstaining hadn't occurred to me?

After confirming that the temperature is to my taste, we're both naked in my giant walk-in shower, making out under the scalding spray. The room is steamy in more ways than one, but I will myself to keep my eyes open no matter what, spellbound by the deep and passionate strokes that we exchange while continuing to grind our erections together.

"Let me get you cleaned up," I suggest, eventually breaking the kiss. With some shower gel in my hand, I kneel before the man who stands with his back inches from the wall, as if he might need support any minute. The man who elicits newfound desires. The man who's sexy as hell and lights a fire in me that has nothing to do with the water temperature. "It's about time I show you how on board I am with us." Ignoring the water splashing down my back, I am pleased to spot a mischievous grin on his gorgeous face.

With his hands splayed on the shower wall behind him, he gives me free rein to touch him however I want. I take great care of every inch of his skin. Running my fingers between his toes, which makes him fidget. Massaging his toned calves. Kneading his firm ass. I stand to carry on with my ministrations. He giggles when my fingers tickle his armpits. This is easy. Don't get me wrong, I touched him all over on the boat, but this has a new meaning and we both know it.

There's no turning back now. My body grows needy. My mind turns filthy. My hand ventures purposefully. Our chests are almost pressed together, and I'm pretty sure he senses the thumping of my heart, as I do his. At once, I grip his length, and when I start stroking him, he drops his head back and groans. Seeing him react like this makes my heart rate soar. Troy takes a step back, his upper body hitting the wall, and he slants his hips so that my other hand can stay on his butt.

Alternatively glancing at my hand tightening its hold on his manhood and my lingering eyes, he clears his throat. "So. Good." I jack him slowly to make it last longer, my thumb rubbing the head teasingly from time to time. He writhes under my touch, and I savor it. I don't want this to end.

"It is… for me, too." In a swift move, my own junk joins the party and I jack us, my eyes expressing everything that I'm not yet ready to voice. His strangled moans boost my ego. I lean into him, sharing what I'm able to for now. "Why I waited so long to touch your cock is beyond me. I have a cock, and touching it is not an issue. I have a cock, and I would have gone ballistic if any of the women I was with had been hesitant to take care of it. I have a cock, and yours feels right in my hand."

He tenses, then croaks out a curse when his release spurts in my wet hand. I follow him shortly after, aroused by how tantalizing I find our masculine pleasure mixed together.

"Hell, yeah!"

CHAPTER 15
DEATH OF ME

Troy

"I can't believe I'm meeting you in person. It's so surreal!" the dark-haired guy exclaims, patting my bicep over my denim jacket, then glancing at Mike in awe. Standing in the entryway, I watch the people dancing, drinking, and munching. Matteo scolded Mike for being late, making Mike's cheeks turn beet red; of course, I put a sock in it.

The sheer size of the penthouse makes the crowd appear smaller than it actually is. Matteo bites the corner of his mouth, then acknowledges that he's been a fan ever since my sound took off on SoundCloud. "I mean, I saw you live at sea, but you're here!" His hands land above my elbow and shake me, as if trying to prevent my disappearance. "This is a completely different… experiment."

Experiment… His accent is subtle, but betrays his Italian heritage. Yet, his choice of words is more fitting when applied to Mike and me.

Mike wants me. He's divulged as much, although he's never wanted a man before. Mike wants me. He's shown as much, although I have to stay his dirty little secret despite touching in ways that would be inconceivable for a straight man. Mike wants me. He's proven as much, although I might only be a temporary experiment. Yeah, for all I know, that's all that I am and ever will be. I involuntarily triggered something in Mike in Paris. Lusting over guys when he believed himself to be straight? Indulging in his curiosity to give guys a try? Pushing self-imposed boundaries with guys? I'm far from complaining, but being introduced as Mike's new friend rankled me... especially when Mike's knuckles brush mine. Beyond his control, I believe. Can't be his form of a silent apology, right?

Why do I sound like Anna's Psych 101 analysis all of a sudden? Why am I so annoyed? Why would he make it official when we're not in a relationship and haven't discussed it? I tend to keep my sexual orientation under wraps because it's not anyone's business. But this isn't my sexual orientation; this is about Mike and me.

Fuck, why am I overthinking this? This isn't like me at all. Overthinking is what took me so long to embrace my attraction to both genders. Overthinking is what made me feel guilty when I jammed my tongue into another boy's mouth. Overthinking is what led me to question who I really am. What a waste of time! I've been called a lot of ugly names in my life, but none were as vile as the labels that I imposed on myself... until I eventually came to terms with who I am. We only have one life after all, and it was about time that I stopped wasting mine.

"Nice to meet you, too." I offer my most convincing "nice guy" smile to Mike's best friend, who gestures at a brunette who could be a Victoria's Secret Angel to join us. "And this is my lovely wife, Luana." We make small talk, and I eventually deduce the origin of her own accent. I'd almost forgotten why Mike was on the Brazil-bound ship in May. "Congratulations, guys... and happy birthday, Matteo!"

I tune them out while they talk about this and that, nodding and smiling at times. It's not Matteo's fault that Mike's uncomfortable with labeling what's going on between us. My teeth clench at the word. At least, I hope he's not… ashamed. My fists curl into a ball, my nails digging into my palms.

Chill out, man, it's barely been six weeks, and you've been out-of-town half the time. He wouldn't have invited you tonight if he were ashamed, the angel on my shoulder reassures me.

But didn't Mike say that he was okay with our situation? Then why hasn't he gone down on you like he said he would at the airport?

I inwardly curse the devil that's been screwing with my head from time to time. The one time that the fool gives it a rest is when Mike's near… but not tonight. Why?

Sighing as discreetly as possible, I glance at the hot piece of man next to me and will my hunger for him to subside so that my eyes won't betray my true intentions. If they linger for too long, Matteo might notice. I can't do that to Mike, although I long for his dick to be in my mouth, like it was right before we got here. Mike isn't quite his usual self either. His body language is more stilted than usual. Maybe he's getting used to the idea of having me around his friends. I need to remember to ask him later; there can't be any secrets between us regarding this particular issue. Whatever it is, he remains unconscious of my inner turmoil. Maybe accepting the invitation here was a bad idea.

"What are the odds that you two became friends?" Mike and I exchange a fleeting glance at Matteo's question and shrug in unison. I'm thankful when Matteo doesn't push the issue, but adds, "What perfect timing! I had no idea that I'd meet Monster Hunter in the flesh while here on business." His voice is edged with excitement. Mike bounces from one foot to the other, pretending to dance to David Guetta's latest hit, even though he loathes electro. "I should have known that July in New York would be brutally hot. Luana doesn't mind, but I do!" He fans himself dramatically, and we talk about the difference between summertime in New York and the Tuscan countryside.

"And you, my traveling friend, remember your Italian summers so well." They exchange a knowing look.

"*Touché.*"

"At least, it gave me an excuse to see you guys again." He and his friend high-five.

"After you ditched us and flew home early, you mean?" Matteo snickers. "I can't believe you did that…" Mike's eyes stare at his feet, then back at his friend. In the blink of an eye, his beautiful face becomes devoid of any emotion. How did he do that? "And all in the name of New York pussy, when I thought you had all you could handle in Brazil!" He winks at Mike to underline his comment, then swirls his tongue inside his mouth, forming an obscene lump on his cheek. Turning his attention to me, Matteo shrugs. "Pardon my French, Monst—."

"Please, Matteo, call me Troy; at least until I'm on stage. My alter ego will take it from there." He nods.

Mike's rushed response comes out a bit too vehemently. "That's absolutely not what it was about, man."

"Right! We Italians know when sex is in the air."

My face falls. He does have a point; Mike's busted like a kid with his hand in the cookie jar… Only he's telling the truth. He fled to meet me, and I'm no pussy.

See, no need to overthink this. I meant enough to him to cut his trip short. He even came to the airport for Christ's sake! Well, I wish that my friend with benefits would tell the entire truth, but now is not the time.

Eager to redirect the conversation, I bombard the newlyweds with questions about this Park Avenue gem that they found on Airbnb and will rent through the end of the year.

"Honey, don't you think Mike and his friend are thirsty? They've been standing here since they arrived because you're monopolizing the conversation."

"Fair point well made, my love. Excuse my shitty manners. Your presence is messing with my head." Matteo's addressing

me, but the weight of Mike's stare isn't lost on me. I wish that
Matteo would chill out; despite my passion and the exposure it
brings, I'm an introvert. "Thanks for making this the best
birthday party ever!" With that, he engulfs me in a friendly hug,
and I stiffen in surprise. When he releases me, he leads us to the
kitchen to get a beer. I don't comment on the fact that bottles of
all types are displayed on a nearby table. I realize how parched I
am when I take a much needed swig. Due to the awkwardness
of my presence, my "friendship" with Mike, my number
one fan.

Matteo clinks the bottom of his beer bottle with mine, and we
drift back to the living room that's officially been converted to
include a makeshift dance floor. Then, he thanks me again,
insisting that I add a certain *je ne sais quoi* while we eat sliders
from the impressive catered buffet. My lips curl upwards at
Matteo's comment, knowing it's useless to argue. Lost in my
thoughts, I shiver. Not from his flattery. Not from the cold. But
from Mike's fingertips brushing my wrist. *What on earth?* His
intimate gesture contradicts how I was introduced. "No need to
be modest. You are Monster Hunter after all!" Flashing me a
supportive smile, he pats my shoulder blade. "So anyway, Troy,
how did you two guys meet?"

*Fuck, I wrongly thought that he'd forgotten about this line of
questioning.*

"Didn't Mike tell you?"

"Actually, he said something that didn't quite make sense.
That's why I'm asking you."

"Thanks for the vote of confidence, dumbass." Mike gives
Matteo shit about his assumption. It gives me the necessary
reprieve to gather my wits.

"And what did Mike tell you?" Somehow, I doubt that Mike
confided about the angry—and hungry—kiss that started this.
What is *this* anyway? I can't find the right label. Who am I to
blame Mike for it, then?

"Something about you bumping into each other and him having no clue who you were. I mean, come on!"

"Well, that's exactly it, Matteo. That's how Mike and I became *friends*... Right, Mike?"

"Would you two stop talking about me like I'm not here?"

Without looking his way, I address my bi-curious "friend" nonetheless. I should probably give Mike a break. We're not dating. I'm not interested in a relationship. He's not prepared to come out after a few weeks... So what's the big deal? I'm full of contradictions and so is he. What a perfect match! I chase the troublesome thought away, returning my focus to how his mixed signals rub me the wrong way.

Must be why I can't help but tease the poor guy. "Nah, it's way too much fun, man." Matteo agrees wholeheartedly. "And just so you know, our *friend,* Mike, here did recognize me." I pin him with my stare. "Right, Mike?"

He grumbles, which I enjoy more than I should; I love teasing him in more ways than one. From the way his eyes narrowed when I said "friend" twice, I know I struck a nerve, similar to when I said "man." But then again, "baby" is reserved for behind closed doors.

Thoughtful, I shrug. " You know, Matteo, sometimes life gives you lemons." Like shitty parents who throw you out of your own home because they can't accept the way you are; I digress. "But along the way, good things happen and sometimes you end up being right were you were supposed to, making new friends." I elbow Mike to force him out of his torpor. What's gotten into him now?

At that, Matteo bites out a bitter laugh, his eyes on Mike, who follows his lead. Furrowing my brows, I try to read between the lines of their unspoken words without success. "So, yeah, we bumped into each other." I repeat in a whisper, enjoying the irony and accuracy of Matteo's phrasing since Mike and I keep bumping into each other willingly, even though I'd rather bump him harder.

"It's hot in here, isn't it?" Matteo's question amuses me. I have no doubt that he noticed my reddening face when that thought crossed my mind.

I'm past embarrassment on so many levels. "It is! Why don't you crack open the window and I'll set up your birthday present?"

Already striding towards the floor-to-ceiling windows with a wide smile plastered on his face, Matteo silently applauds what's to come; his admiration warms my heart.

When he's out of earshot, Mike leans my way and utters, "As soon as you're done with your set, we're out of here."

Concern constricts my chest. "Was I out of line? I'll behave." On impulse, the back of my hand reaches for his cheek.

His face blanches, and he snatches my wrist so strongly that I wince. "How can you be so blind?" he stammers, and I'm at a loss. "I... I need to..." His gaze skims over my body, his lewd expression shooting straight to my dick, which strains against my zipper.

"You need to what?" I ask within a breath, knowing his answer will distract me from my upcoming performance.

"Fuck you."

CHAPTER 16
BEAST OF BURDEN

Mike

"You could have at least waited for us to be in the car!" Troy's voice bounces off of the elevator's steel walls as he readjusts his trademark cowboy hat on his stubborn head and presses the button for the ground floor.

At his tone, I swivel my head hoping to catch his eye, but he won't allow it. His jaw ticks, and I swear that I can hear him grinding his teeth. *What the fuck is wrong with him?* "What prompted your foul mood?" He's been acting weird ever since I suggested that we bail and skip the rest of the party.

"Oh, please! You've got to be kidding me, Mike. I screwed up my performance because of you." He points at me while toying with his belt with his free hand. Glaring at me, he growls, "You say things and don't deal with the consequences."

My cheeks are on fire, and I inhale deeply to calm myself. "Excuse me?"

"See…" His finger approaches my face accusingly. "You're doing it again."

"Doing what, Troy? Your performance was great. Everyone danced, cheered, and applauded. Matteo's beyond thrilled. I bet he's filing for divorce as we speak to marry you and benefit from your talents." I burst out laughing, knowing that my innuendos probably aren't welcome, but I have to try to lighten the mood.

"Ha-ha." He takes off his hat and runs his fingers through his disheveled hair before putting it back on. "Dammit! You can't look at me like I'm your favorite meal and the next second have this… this mask that you hide behind and tell me to fuck off like it's totally normal," he snarls. "My head wasn't in the game while I was DJing, and you're to blame, jackass."

"Troy, you're not making any sense." I manage to intercept his hand that's flying all over the place. Brushing his knuckle with my thumb, I clutch his fisted hand. "Baby, that didn't happen. Even months ago when I probably should have cussed you out, I never did. Believe me, I'm not about to start now. I said, 'I need to fuck you.' You were so hyper that you misunderstood."

"You've been hot and cold all night. It's only been a few weeks, so I get that you need time before telling your friends about us. I played by your rules. Then you touch me." He leans against the mirrored rear of the car and crosses his legs at the ankles. "Nothing obvious, of course, but you broke the rules. You're jerking me around, and I didn't sign up for this."

"What do you want from me, Troy? I'm new to this." I alternatively point to him and myself. "You've been attracted to guys your whole life."

He cuts me off, his chocolate eyes daring me to react. "And girls."

With my poker face on, I nod, flashing back to when I bumped into him while he was lip-locked with a woman. We don't delve into specifics, and I don't really care, to be honest. I want *him*. Who he fucked in the past doesn't matter; this is a conversation for another time. Another place. Another state of mind. "Listen, I hear you, Troy. I'm sorry if I broke what we'd established… To be honest, I can't help but touch you. I want you so bad! That's why I told you that I needed to fuck you. I meant it… Apparently, you have no idea how sexy you are and how horny *you* make me. So, yes, I mean it. Anal will be the test. According to Google, it'll need some prep. That's fine by me. Either way, I need to fuck you or you to fuck me, whichever you prefer, since we haven't discussed the technicalities yet. I am *very* serious."

Thank God, that stupefies him, making his jaw drop to a point where it looks detached from the rest of his face… unless the Picasso impression is due to whatever it was that I smoked while he was DJing.

I can't stand his ridiculous complaint, though. He needs to comprehend that he doesn't run the show. In a split second, I slam the emergency stop button, abruptly stopping our descent, and invade his personal before he can protest.

Damn, he's gorgeous.

"Troy, as much as I appreciate your smart mouth, now is not the time to be a diva. Your show was great. You need to chill the fuck out. Now let me work my magic." My mouth collides with his, forcefully requiring entrance. Unabashedly rubbing my shaft against his, I awkwardly slip my hand into the small space between his back and the cabin and knead his ass, eventually peeling my body from his to make quick work of his belt and lower his zipper. His earlier resistance is nowhere to be found. Meanwhile, our tongues dance. It's a rare occurrence for both of us to be clean-shaven. His lips are more forceful somehow, like he's trying to compensate for the difference. Unless I am.

His lingering anger fuels the arousal humming in my blood. Before breaking to come up for air, I swat the side of his butt and congratulate myself when he takes the hint, shifts his pelvis, and lets me make quick work of his pants. They fall to his ankles in a thump when his belt hits the floor. That's my cue to drop to my knees in front of him.

Troy's eyes cage me; they're glazed with lust. "You don't have to do this."

"Do you have any idea how much I want this? I may not be quite ready for more yet, but…" I trail off. My fingertips begin a teasing journey from his ankle to his muscular thigh, tracing imaginary patterns. His hands clench the railing behind him, and he shivers under my touch. "I love every part of your body, Troy Hunter." The palm of my hand reaches his throbbing erection that's hidden under the fabric of his black boxer briefs.

I'm responsible for this, which makes my heart swell with pride and joy. Caressing him, there's no fear in my heart as I watch him harden. I lick my lips in anticipation, baffled when my mouth waters.

Why was I hesitant this whole time?

His taut frame slumps a bit, and a sly smile forms at the corner of his lips when my fingers grip the waistband of his boxer briefs and set him free. My heart skips a beat. I stick my tongue out to wet the pad of my thumb and gently circle the head of his cock, which pulsates with every stroke. Who would have thought that another guy's package could be such a turn-on? "You are so beautiful."

A deep chuckle escapes his sexy mouth. He mouths a thank you that settles deep in my gut. Matteo's words from earlier tonight come to mind. Words that made me touch him before I could stop myself.

Yes, Troy, you brought an extra je ne sais quoi *into my life, and I wouldn't want it any other way.*

Soon enough, the tip of my tongue replaces my thumb and I get acquainted with his masculine scent that drives me crazy. Let the frenzy begin!

Why was I hesitant this whole time?

While my tongue swirls around his crown, my hand circles his girth, finding a rhythm as I jerk him off. Maintaining eye contact, I apply the pressure that I'd enjoy, hoping that he does, too. My answer comes in the form of a thunderous grunt. That's all the encouragement I need to take him in my mouth, although I'm incapable of deep-throating like he does. I guess it takes practice; I'm up for the challenge.

He squeezes his eyes shut for a moment, his head falling back against the metal panel. All this time, he bucks his pelvis and moves in time with my ministrations.

Occasionally, I release him with a popping sound that lightens the charged air.

"Such a tease, you are." We breathe in sync.

I kiss his tip and witness his reaction with bliss. "Yup!" I wink and carry on with my TLC. He mumbles something that I don't catch over all the little noises we make.

Each time my hand gets close to his balls, my thumb rubs them. It's so fucking arousing to make a grown-ass man moan. The more I suck him, the more I stop analyzing my actions. My brain is disconnected from my body, or rather hyperconnected, considering my boner. My free hand that grasped the back of his thigh for balance flies to my crotch. As much as I wish I could relieve the agonizing pressure, touching myself while blowing him would be stupid. My focus is on him. My tongue plays with him. My hand torments him. My own release can wait, although I might end up creaming my pants like a preteen; who cares? For now, all that matters is Troy. And, yes, I'm turned on like never before. From blowing a guy. Nah, blowing this particular guy. My guy?

"Oh, fuck!" His fingers tangle in my hair. "I... Yeah... do that again." I oblige, running my tongue along his length while softly pinching his balls. "Harder."

With that, he moves faster and loses all semblance of control. My pulse races when I feel him tightening against my fingers. My name rolling off his tongue sends me into overdrive, and I don't back away when he warns me that he's close. Now is not the time to chicken out, right?

We lock eyes as he stills, sweat trickling down his temple. Unfazed by my decision, I drink every drop of him. Unfazed by his taste, I lick my lips to tease him some more. Unfazed by our attraction, I finally grasp that Troy means more to me than I care to admit. Spent, his next words are barely audible, but the air shifts as my eyes remain glued to him while I blindly search for the button to restart the elevator.

Why was I hesitant this whole time?

"Only you."

CHAPTER 17
COME WAKE ME UP

Troy

"You're welcome to join me, you know." Pressing my elbow on the mattress, I will myself to rise above the lethargy. Supporting my head with my splayed palm, I lie on my left side, my hungry eyes roaming over his appetizing body. The view is partially blocked since we're wearing boxer briefs to keep from going at it again. That's what we've been doing all day, and it's past five now. What a great way to spend a Saturday!

I don't think I'll ever tire of the spectacular view; yes, he's hot as fuck, but most of all, he's become such an essential part of my life.

A satisfied grin on his face, Mike catches his breath, lying on his back in my bed, where we spent our lazy day. The last one of September, which means that next week's my birthday, and I'm debating whether to disclose that piece of information. Does he even care?

Eyes closed, his fingers are laced behind his head. I take him in, memorizing how he looks at this very moment, as if he'd vanish out of thin air or ghost me like he once did. It may be stupid, but this nagging notion keeps rearing its ugly head. Not today.

His light brown hair has grown longer and wavier over the last few months, lessening the resemblance to Channing Tatum. Unless it's because I now know the real Michael Clayton, despite being away every so often for a gig.

"Nah, I think I'll pass this time. Plus, I already have dinner plans with Matteo." Mike rolls onto his stomach and attacks my lips like his life depends on it. One kiss and I was hooked. Funny how our kisses always have an extra *je ne sais quoi*, as Matteo would say.

When he resumes his position, I take a wild guess. "You afraid to meet my new friends or what? Or is it because Studio 45 isn't a *regular* club?" Of course, I air quote the word I picked to sidestep what I actually meant: straight. Funny that I told him that there shouldn't be any taboo words between us, but I can't seem to follow my own rule.

At once, he grabs the bottle of water that I left on the nightstand, takes a swig, then mirrors my posture. A smile crinkles the corners of his green eyes. "You've told me so much about Studio 45 that I'd love to see it with my own eyes, even though I'm not into the music." Yeah, Mike's been open about dislike of electro, which he associates with club music. "I'm sorry I always have prior engagements when you invite me." He ruffles my hair, his hand settling on my cheek next. Out of reflex, his thumb caresses my neck behind my ear. I used to hate these displays of affection. I crave them with Mike, but you'd have to torture me to grant it. "Honestly, Claire and her purple dreadlocks sound like a lot of fun. As for her friend, Drake, thanks to your description of Dracula on steroids, I decided that he's a fictional character." I snicker at that. "I wonder when this meetup is going to happen now that my dream job's taking up all my time!"

I congratulated him when he landed it two weeks ago; it's not every day that a famous fashion designer calls you with good news. Mike stressed that his parents' connections had nothing to do with it. It's cute how he stubbornly ignores how names can also open doors. I'm not saying that he doesn't deserve the job; his sketches prove that he's freaking talented. Anyway, I'm happy that he's happy and won't comment on the luxury that he could afford to stay unemployed this long without financial issues. I could've done the same to some extent if I'd followed my parents' rules. *No, thank you...* But I digress.

"Why don't I meet your friends after work next week?" Yeah, I, too, have a steady job. I opted to play it safe. Though gigs can bring good money, experience has told me that there's no guarantee it'll last. Money's always been a thorn in my side, and I'm glad that my head's not in the clouds or I might have burned through it already instead of investing it in my Park Slope apartment.

Over time, the post-contract craziness wore off and I settled into a new routine. I travel at least once a week and my sound remains popular, but bartending part-time offers enough flexibility to juggle my two favorite nighttime activities. Neither gives me the opportunity to use my degree in management, yet I'm hoping it'll eventually work to my advantage with my DJ activities—I wish I could call it a career, but I'm not there yet...

The feel of his warm breath on my face depletes my self-control. I can't refrain anymore when his coveting gaze becomes heated at the sight of how he affects me. "Well, my crazy friends are super busy with the tattoo parlor. Guess they don't have a life outside of it..." Explaining what I know of how they took over for the original owner, I kiss his face after every three or four words, and my resolve to get out of bed crumbles accordingly. "Besides letting loose and dancing at the club, that is."

"Seeing their tattoos with my own eyes intrigues me."

"Mmm... Funny that their tats come up every time we discuss them. Is there something I should know? I mean, your skin's got no trace of ink." I arch my brow that I've considered piercing with a barbell to spice up my DJ look. Two things stopped me: such a visible piercing might not fit my cowboy persona and my employer at the bar doesn't allow visible piercings. So, that'll have to wait, although Claire said that she'll keep a spot open for me. "Now, curious minds need to know: barbell on your nipple or tribal tat around your bicep?"

He shivers and pouts before hiding his lingering anguish with his signature poker face.

"I'm sorry. Did I say something wrong?" My hand reaches for said bicep. "That was meant as a joke. You know that, right?"

"Yeah... No... I..."

I tighten my hold on his arm and shake it. "You're clamming up again." He can't react like this and expect me to drop it, can he? "Talk to me, Mike."

He swallows with a strangled noise, lowers his beautiful green eyes for a split second, and sighs when they raise to mine. "I'm the one who should apologize." He pecks my cheek. "Apparently, I'm still not over it."

"Over what?"

And just like that, our mundane conversation about my heavily tattooed friends shifts to a heavier one that I didn't anticipate. With great difficulty, he confesses how his childhood dream got crushed in a millisecond when the young prodigy fell off his horse during an equestrian competition that he was favored to win. Countless painful surgeries helped save his right leg—plastic surgery erased most of the scars—but he couldn't walk and was sent to a private clinic in Switzerland, where his boarding school was.

"That's how I met Matteo, who had been in a terrible car wreck. We bonded over physical therapy while my father resented me from afar." He shrugs, tears welling in his beautiful eyes.

Hurt settles in his facial features; for once, he doesn't try to hide his emotions that he obviously considers a weakness. He wipes the threatening tears with his forearm. The loud sigh that follows sounds more relieved than the previous one.

"My father's a despicable person, but my mom's kinda my best friend. Shrinks said it shouldn't be that way, but it works for us, so screw them! She leads a hectic life and I don't get to see her much, but I think she always felt the need to compensate for his lack of humanity."

Wow, Mike's old man sounds like a carbon copy of my parents. Bastards!

I hope that's not where the connection I instantly felt with Mike lies.

Nah, we put our chemistry to the test. Parents are out of the equation, sort of.

I can tell that he isn't interested in my pity, nor that I broadcast my own trauma. He knows we all have our own shit to deal with.

It's a slippery slope, though. Guarded Mike took another shaky step towards me, and I salute his bravery. Wary of saying the wrong thing after he revealed something so intimate, I wait to find an opening to lighten the mood. Teasing him about some of his expressions is one of my favorite pastimes. It's my way of proving that I pay attention to everything he says. The thing is, neither of us seems to be motivated to share too many personal details. My knee-jerk reaction the first time I saw his place on 11th Street led to a short convo about his big-shot criminal lawyer dad and privileged international upbringing after his parents' divorce. To reciprocate, I simply said that my parents weren't in the picture anymore. It led him to believe that they were dead, which isn't far from the truth. That's enough for now.

"Hence, I hate needles. So, I'll admire tats and piercings from a distance."

"Did you truly say '*hence*'? Who says things like that?"

"I do, asshole." His large frame covers mine, and he trails open-mouth kisses across my bare chest. At once, the traitor grips the pillow behind him and throws it at me. I welcome the assault and fight back with all I've got.

Minutes later, his hearty laugh warms my heart. He murmurs a thank you.

"Anytime, baby." I stroke his hand with my thumb.

"You know, I've been thinking about our conversation in the car, after Matteo's birthday. I thought it would take more time for me to come to terms with my attraction to you. I know I freaked out at first because you're a dude. But I like what we have, and that's more important than your gender. I mean it. If the rest of the world doesn't like my choices, so be it. So… here's my take on the situation. I learned to live with a bigoted father; I'll learn to deal with sideway glares, offensive comments, and judgmental strangers. It might not be easy, but I'm ready. I switched careers to be happier. Switching teams to be with you has made be happier, too, so far. This is my life. I'm done pleasing others."

I kiss his forehead, then watch his chest muscles tense, biting my lip to suppress the need to lick his skin.

Damn, I can't keep my hands and other body parts off of him… Well, one body part remains clueless as to when it'll have the chance to take his virginity. That's a topic we haven't broached since he decided that we should stay at my place for a change… after his first of many blowjobs, which was other-worldly.

All the more reason not to push my luck. The fact that Mike talks about fucking me, or me fucking him, without his eyes drifting away means that he's getting accustomed to the prospect. At times, my craving becomes overwhelming and I almost cave. Then, I remember that I shouldn't be selfish; it should be his call.

So far, he's timidly initiated things, which I'm grateful for. To say that ass play comes naturally would be far-fetched.

When two guys get naked, that's bound to happen. Nothing wrong with that. One of the perks of being attracted to dudes is that they're basically horny 24/7, so you might as well take advantage of it, right?

One step at a time. Fingers. One step at a time. Ass. One step at a time. Prostate. Why is the world ruled by men who believe that dicks are the ultimate power when it's blatant that prostates bring you mind-blowing, stars-in-your-eyes orgasms? This world's priorities are definitely upside down.

Well, not really. Mike is mine at the moment, and let me tell you, Mike is one horny beast when he shuts down that over-worked brain of his. The one that instills the guilt. The one that questions what his friends would think. The one that dares to underestimate what we have. He jokes about how fucking tight I am and how he has no clue how he'll fit; I wasn't joking when I said Big Dick Richie fit him better than Magic Mike. Jokes aside, I can appreciate his desire and apprehension. Life's taught me to be patient, and I'm in no hurry. The fact that I'm his dirty little secret doesn't bode well.

We're good together. Why hide? Why pretend? Why wait? Suddenly, words that I probably should have said earlier tumble out of my stupid mouth. "You know I haven't been with anyone else since I met you, right?"

"Why are you telling me this?"

I thread my fingers through my hair, staring into his fierce eyes. "I should have made it abundantly clear much sooner. I'm not after a relationship, but I don't play the field either."

"Okay." He pecks my cheek again.

"That's it?" My brows knit.

"Let's make a deal, Troy Hunter. You hate labels and some scare me. So first, no label for what's going on between us which, to me, is a relationship, no matter how hard I fought against it and you still are. Second, no label for my sexual orientation when I come out to Matteo later tonight."

"Deal."

CHAPTER 18
TRUE COLORS

Mike

Nursing my Guinness, I glance at Matteo while the famous jazz club near my place gets busier by the second. I'm more of a rock and 50's classics fan, but his love of jazz knows no bounds, same with electro. He shares the former with my mom and the latter with his wife. Me? I'm happy to tag along, although my clammy hands are a clear indication that I'm lying to myself. How pitiful!

Oblivious to my discomfort, my friend shoots a text to Luana; I admire how the newlyweds make solo time for their friends. Chuckling at how different my younger, infatuated self acted with Ella, I guzzle my beer.

His double bass in hand, the artist is about to begin, and I sigh at my cowardice.

Where to start? What to say? How to confess?

Grinning my way, Matteo shuts off his phone and puts it face down on the small round table that's covered with a thick white tablecloth, embroidered with the club's monogram. He focuses on the music and I feign to do the same, but my mind is running a mile a minute.

During intermission, my Italian friend shoots me an odd look.

I purse my lips and snap, "What?" My index finger circles the rim of my empty beer glass.

Instead of responding, he swivels to catch the tall waitress's attention and orders sparkling water without bothering to ask what I want.

When she's gone, his attention returns to me. "You tell me." His joined hands land on the edge of the table. "You've been awfully quiet for someone who sounded so eager to see me. I gave you ample time to spill the beans, but all I see is your nervous habits. So… You. Tell. Me." His piercing eyes bore into mine, and despite the dim light, I feel exposed.

This is it.

The chianti that we enjoyed with our gnocchi dinner didn't help to loosen my nerves, neither did the Guinness.

"You're really perceptive, you know."

"Shocker!" His right hand splays over his heart before he resumes his position. "Isn't that what got us talking when we were both kids?"

"True." I break eye contact to gather my thoughts and sigh. When I raise my eyes to his, I announce, "I met someone," and catch my breath, grumbling at my shaky voice. My throat is parched, and I welcome the sparkling water that the waitress deposits on the table at the right moment to grant a brief reprieve. Only now do I notice how hot she is. We exchange a flirtatious yet harmless smile.

My initial confusion regarding my sexual orientation after being attracted to Troy and being turned-on by gay porn was quickly resolved; good old straight porn remains equally arousing. Although most would argue that I'm too old to indulge in adult movies, Brandon Boner's non-trashy ones did the trick. Troy scoffed when he managed to weasel this information out of me one drunken night.

Anyway, I've come to terms with discovering that I'm bi. It's time to spell it out loud to make it a reality. Why am I so jumpy? My sexual orientation is a part of me, but it doesn't define me. I'm still me.

"Must be someone important." As always, Matteo's spot-on. His voice is gleeful and collected. I must be imagining the hint of pain in it. "Because it's not like you to keep things under wraps, especially with me." My silence hurt him! Fuck!

Suddenly, I'm at a loss for words. I nod and sip on my water to soothe my aching throat... and buy a few more precious seconds. He offers a small smile and drinks as well. "So, where did you meet this *important someone?*" Playful, he air quotes his last words.

"On the cruise ship." My thumb and index finger roll the fabric of the tablecloth; it's a good thing that he can't see this from where he sits.

"Ohhh... Now, I'm even more intrigued." One of his eyebrows spikes up.

I snicker at his scrutiny, wishing that the next band would move faster while prepping their instruments and the stage for their performance.

"To be honest, I had a feeling that you found a hook-up on the ship. You always seemed to be... otherwise occupied, but you didn't say anything, so I had no clue it kept going after we landed. Especially with Stella and—" He abruptly stops and gulps the remainder of his beverage. "Sorry, I'm babbling. What I meant to say is: It's been a while since you've met someone that mattered to you. I'm happy for you, man." He pats my forearm a couple of times. "Too bad I didn't get a chance to meet your *important someone.*" Air quotes are back, which makes me chuckle. His agitation betrays his excitement at the news, which I find endearing.

"Well, actually, you guys met."

He rubs his chin between his thumb and index finger while

mine have stopped wrinkling the tablecloth. "Is this the girl who looked like Margot Robbie?" He missed my subtle hint, thinking of the first woman he saw me with on the cruise.

Swallowing the lump in my throat, I take notice of my throbbing pulse and take a deep breath, making a point to look him in the eye while shaking my head.

"It's not a girl... or a woman, for that matter." I let out a heavy sigh. Now, I've said it without leaving any room for ambiguity!

My friend doesn't even blink or comment on my flushed face. "What's his name?"

"His name's Troy," I say, seeing the wheels turn in Matteo's head. Mentioning Troy's name sends the right kind of shivers down my spine as naughty thoughts from earlier today invade my mind.

"Do I have to beg for you to clue me in?"

Despite my stiff neck, I tilt my head backwards laughing.

"Can I at least get a hint?"

Now, this is too easy. "Cowboy hat."

Matteo's eyes bug like a cartoon character. He leans closer. "Ha-ha! Monster Hunter, right?" I can tell that he doesn't believe me. He shrugs. "Fine, have it your way, keep your secret." He leans back in his chair.

"Troy Hunter *was* my secret, Matteo, but now, you know." *Damn, it feels good to have everything out in the open!* "It started out..." I run my fingers through my hair while deciding how to phrase this. "We started talking after a misunderstanding. It didn't take long for me to be genuinely attracted to him. We..." I cough. "Made out. Trust me, I had a hard time—in more ways than one—wrapping my head around the idea of being physical with a dude. Although nobody knew, a part of me still rebelled against it. After some back and forth, we knew it was more than that." It's my turn to shrug.

A completely unfazed Matteo simply states, while reaching

to circle my wrist, "It's about time you found someone you love." Then, he adds, "I wish you'd told me earlier, though. And by earlier, I don't mean during dinner. From the look on your face tonight, I could tell that something was up. Granted, I wouldn't have guessed. But, come on, Mike! It's me, Matteo!" His index finger points inward at his chest.

"I know, I should have said something sooner." I look away, then back at him. "I guess I needed to figure out what was going on before I could speak the words, you know?" I'm back to wrinkling the tablecloth when I admit, "If I'm completely honest, I was anxious about your reaction... because your acceptance means more than you can imagine."

He releases his hold. "I'm not sure I follow your train of thought. You don't need my blessing, Mike. *You* need to fully accept what's going on with your life right now. I'm actually a little hurt. As if I'd judge you! Again, it's not about me, man. It's about you. After all we've been through, you're still hesitant to speak your mind. I don't know if your jackass of a dad is to blame, but you're twenty-seven and it's time to grow up. What people do behind closed doors is nobody else's business, right? Unless I bring it up myself, you don't need to know if I'm into vanilla sex or not." Then the fucker raises his eyebrow as if daring me to ask! "Just like I don't give a shit if you top or bottom."

I swat his arm for good measure, and we laugh together, as we often do.

Yeah, Matteo's always to the point; I don't disclose where Troy and I stand in that department... Nobody else's business! But hiding it proves that I wasn't comfortable. I don't want to broadcast it, but faking it is even worse. No matter how right Troy and I feel. No matter how stupid I had been to conceal it. No matter how wary I was of my friends' reactions. I have to accept who I am. Even if it doesn't last, this relationship is a part of me, and if I pretend that it doesn't matter, I risk losing it. I can't let that happen. I can't deny how much I care about Troy. I can't lie to myself. Otherwise, my asshole of a dad, like Matteo called him, would have won. I would be denying myself in order to please others.

You should have seen my father's angular face blanche when I told him that I'd applied to become a fashion designer instead of working at his law firm! All my narrow-minded father could focus on was that all men in fashion were supposedly "gays and drug addicts." The irony isn't lost on me, considering my current relationship. Spending time with Troy taught me to slowly but surely embrace who I truly am the way that he does. How could I, of all people, forget that life's too short to let others dictate your life?

"Aren't you a bit jealous that I'm 'having an affair' with your favorite celeb?" It's my turn to air quote and be playful, which is refreshing. Finding the appropriate words to describe our situation remains a struggle.

"Sure am!" The asshole mocks me nonetheless when I eventually confess the revenge kisses, the undeniable chemistry, and the uncanny serendipity.

Thank God, Matteo wasn't there to witness my first encounter with the cowboy bartender; I'm mortified enough that acquaintances who called themselves friends saw that! Thinking about it, I grin like the moron that I am; I'm okay disclosing tidbits, but I'm definitely not ready to share how that unforgettable kiss happened.

"Story of your life, Mike! Life brought you lemons, and you ended up where you were meant to be, making unlikely friends... or lovers." Again, I keep my big mouth shut; Troy and I aren't quite lovers, but why fight the inevitable? "Actually, it all makes sense now! I held myself back from saying something when I felt the heat between you guys, but you said he was a friend, so..." *Why do my shoulders tense?* "Chill out, man. I know you by heart; I notice things. You weren't ready to explain an attraction that you didn't understand yourself. I get that. It's not my place to say this, but I don't care. You said you envy my stability as a married man. Well, trust my experience with Luana; you and Troy make more sense than you ever did with Ella." *Why does this make me happy?* "High school sweethearts. Four-year relationship. Almost engaged." *Why does it take this conversation to make me realize that my own story resembles that of my parents?* "When I met Ella, my first thought was that you were in love with the idea of love." *Why does he use the same words my mom did to describe the reason behind marrying my father so young?* "I didn't get those vibes at my birthday party... See, Love Boat effect!"

Love Boat, my ass... I've told Troy countless times that he's fucking sexy and I love what we have. But I'm not in love with Troy. It's too much. It's too soon. It's too... impossible!

The more I deny my sentiments, the more he counters. And that's okay.

I'm lucky to have a witty and supportive friend like Matteo Moretti in my life.

The best.

CHAPTER 19
HEAVEN UPSIDE DOWN

Mike

S ifting through the glass bowl where I keep my keys and
miscellaneous items in the entryway for the umpteenth
time, I grunt yet again. My murderous glare turns
toward the staircase. "Mom! I can't find my car keys," I growl
but doubt she can hear me from the guest floor where Chet
Baker's blaring. Oh well. No matter how much her scattered
nature annoys me, I enjoy having her around. I haven't seen
enough of her since getting back from France... Well, Brazil.
She got here while I was swamped at work yesterday, so I've
decided to treat her tonight, even though I usually stay home on
weekdays.

"Stop yelling, Michael. Will you? I'll be right down." As
always, her voice is chipper, but collected. It has the ability to
calm my temper and keep me grounded.

My colorful mother saunters down the steps with a wide
smile plastered on her full face; she considers climbing the
flights of stairs to the guest floor while having a phone conversation exercise. Colorful due to the mix of colors she enjoys wearing, although some might call it questionable. Seriously, though,

I wouldn't want my mom to be any other way. We call her style hippie chic to piss off my uptight father.

Standing on the last step to compensate for the difference in height, she pecks my cheek. "I'm sorry I kept you waiting, I was reading another article about the recent murders in the Boston area. You fit the victim profile, so I don't want you visiting me for a while."

"Mom, come on. I've heard the news and it's bullshit, folklore at best. There are things the media's not telling us; no one can turn someone into a mummy nowadays! Can we move on with our lives and enjoy the evening?"

"Well, you shouldn't take things for granted. Plus, I can't help it! You know my morbid fascination with this headline news." My mom touches her perfectly styled red hair and beams at me. "Okay, I'm ready." She sighs and ruffles my hair. "You're even more handsome with your hair this way." Before I have time to dismiss the compliment, she asks, "So, where are you taking me?"

"There's a new bistro nearby I thought we could give a try. Maybe afterwards, we can hit a jazz club that Matteo and I discovered."

"Perfect idea, Michael. You're so thoughtful." Yeah, she's well aware that jazz isn't my thing. Thanks to Troy's influence, I've broadened my horizons music-wise, amongst other things. His patience wears thin whenever I can't make it through a full electro or country song. At first, I wondered if the cowboy hat was an act. In time, I fathomed that it was a part of him he usually hides and his penchant for techno overshadowed his diverse tastes in music. His passion for country music shocked me, although I knew he grew up in Texas. Not all Texans enjoy country music, right? He blushed when he said that he trusted me enough to disclose it, which made me laugh.

Sharing my childhood trauma with Troy was liberating, and our relationship took another step in the direction of steady. He may fight the evidence, but it's useless. I found it utterly endearing when he eventually stopped hiding his natural twang. He claims that the world's a stage, so he practiced hiding his accent and sometimes forgets how he originally sounds. It's pretty funny when it slips. Why am I not surprised that my thoughts are drifting his way yet again?

I rub the back of my neck, avoiding her gaze. She's immune to my poker face and can read me like an open book. There's so much I've kept to myself. There's so much I'm debating whether to confess. There's so much I need to get off my chest. I'm so hyper lately that she must think I'm a nervous wreck because of my new job. "It's been a while since we'd been on a mother and son date. I've missed you, Mom."

"I've missed you, too." Her spontaneous embrace is as big as her heart. "Here." Releasing me, she searches her pants pocket and proudly produces my key, lifting her arm so they hang at eye level; I can't remember when she was taller than me! "You do the driving. I took a spin to the charity auction while you were at work, but meh... It seems that I can't handle New York traffic after all. My area's much quieter."

"How can you even compare a residential area of Boston to Manhattan?"

"My point exactly. Come on, I'm starving," she declares and steps down to the hardwood floor, leading the way to the garage.

Technically, we could have walked to the bistro and the jazz club, but the drizzle that's lingered these past few days is plain annoying and I'd rather stay dry.

You see, I made plans to surprise Troy for his birthday weekend, including ordering a carrot cake from a bakery; I learned that it's his favorite thanks to his ridiculous this or that game. How could he know that I shamelessly studied the ID he discarded on the island counter when we stayed at his place last weekend? We were too busy making out all day.

Thoughtful, I follow my mom after grabbing both of our

coats on the way. A smirk reaches the corner of my mouth as I remember how my evening with Matteo unfolded. Per usual, my friend saw right through me and didn't buy any of my initial pretenses. In a way, he resembles my mom. Trustworthy. Honest. Loving. But will coming out to her be as easy as it was with my best friend? Nah, strike that, that wasn't easy, *Matteo* made it easy.

When I pull out of the garage, my mother glances my way and asks if I'm all right. "I'm fine, Ma. It's the brutal cold."

"Right…" I don't miss her dubious tone, but play dumb.

Once we get to the restaurant, my inner turmoil takes over, and when I'm rendered speechless, my chatty mother gladly fills in the blanks. Her uneventful second marriage. Her life in Weston, Massachusetts. Her lack of regrets regarding Edward Clayton, who gave her a son that she adores. Half a bottle of wine later, she confesses that I was a surprise baby; for the first time, she mentions a specific health condition that made her less likely to get pregnant.

"You were a miracle baby, Michael. I love you with all my heart, and I sincerely hope that you'll become someone else's miracle. Finding that one person that matters. For real."

While indulging in a piece of delicious cheesecake, we discuss ordinary miracles. Before I know it, my busy mind drifts to the person who barged in on my life without so much as a warning label.

I eventually feel the weight of my mom's stare and venture, "How do you know when you're in love?"

Her hand covers mine and squeezes it before her gaze flicks my way. She offers me a wide smile that reaches the corners of her blue eyes. "Oh, Michael…"

"What?" I narrow my gaze to decipher the emotion behind her strangled voice.

She clears her throat and gulps what's left in her glass. Sighing, she releases my hand and pins me with her penetrating gaze.

"There's no universal definition. There's hunger, attraction, and chemistry, of course, but as far as I'm concerned, 'in love' is slightly different." She air quotes the expression. "Being *in love* with someone is putting the person first. I'm not saying that you should deny who you are, quite the opposite... It means that someone else matters in your choices. For no apparent reason, you know and love their little idiosyncrasies. Things that might bother you if it were anybody else, you know. For example, you're so attuned that when the person enters the room, you sense it without looking. It's not about compromising, taking things for granted, or needing the person to complete you. It's about no-brainer agreements, easy communication, and effortless balance."

What a wise and wonderful person my mother is! I nod, wishing I could order some alcohol to process her answer and instantly regretting that I'm the designated driver. "Thanks." I wrongly think that this concludes the topic.

Her fingers drum on the small round table. "Are you in love with someone, Michael?" Her voice softens and her eyes glisten.

Her question knocks the wind out of me. Yes, I am totally, gleefully, and insanely on board with these feelings that I've never experienced before. As I am with all of the sensations that Troy ignites in me. As I am with sharing the most mundane things with him, like cooking our veggie omelets in the morning. As I am with waking up next to him, although I hadn't envisioned a future with a man. Especially one who claims he doesn't do relationships and lives for the nightlife that I don't care for. I don't want this to end. I don't want him to get bored with me. I don't want him to think that he's a phase.

Oh, fuck!

I make a point to maintain eye contact. "You just made me realize that I am."

"I'm so happy for you, Michael." My heart soars as she awkwardly reaches over the table to hug me. "Now, I know why

I felt something was different about you," she murmurs into my ear. "There's no reason to be nervous, though." Oh, she felt that, too! She resumes her position. "Love should rule the world, Michael." I chuckle at that; if only it were so simple. "So, what's his name?"

I gawk, although it takes my brain a moment to realize that she *knows*. How? I'm not embarrassed. I'm not ashamed. I'm in love. Damn! Matteo was right.

"Troy Hunter."

CHAPTER 20
HERE TONIGHT

Troy

M y face softens as I gaze at the breathtaking man waiting for the elevator next to me. "You blew this completely out of proportion, you know."

Mike's hand covers mine; then he laces his fingers with mine. I tighten my hold. He whispers into my ear, "Not blowing anything except you as soon as we get back to our room." A heated expression flashes across his face, followed by a mix of amazement and... awe? I'm doing a piss-poor job of reading him, especially when he baffles me by lifting our joined hands and kissing my knuckles without checking whether someone's watching. Scratching his neck with his free hand, he sighs, contentment now written all over his face.

His carefree attitude warms my heart. I can't believe how eagerly he's embraced what he keeps calling our *relationship*. I'm not sure exactly what defines a relationship. Time together? Nah, I've been with people longer than Mike. Good sex? Nah, I've had meaningless sex with people more than once. Overlapping interests? Nah, I've made a list and they couldn't be more opposite. Whatever it is, it works. It's not forced, it's meaningful, and I think we're both pushing boundaries while having fun together. His surprise birthday present is yet another example, as was the fact that he managed to talk to my manager and arrange a day off from work to make it happen. How cool is that?

"You mean the place that's three times bigger than my apartment? Honestly, Mike, this is too much." I sigh at the crowd around us, wishing that I could hold him hostage in the elevator like after Matteo's party. My body hums at the memory, and I make a mental note to attempt a repeat as we step into the cabin that'll take us to the Palazzo Tower chairman suite and its three bedrooms. A must-have, according to him, and a dent in his trust fund to benefit from the private pool, sauna, and spa, as well as the terrace. "Way too much!" When we stumbled into the suite last night, following a first-class flight, a frisky Mike insisted that we christen each room. He claims that it's simply an excuse to get me naked for the entire three-day weekend. Unsurprisingly, we've opted for room service, apart from tonight's early dinner prior to the concert, that is.

So far, we've stuck to his plan and haven't seen much of Vegas. The view that I most appreciate occurs whenever we—almost—have sex. One step at a time, right? I remember what he said about anal being the real test; we're not there yet. Don't get me wrong, I adore what we have, but that'll prove whether we're truly compatible. All in due time.

"I wish I could've been there for your first time in Vegas." Between the first-class flight, gigantic suite, and prime tickets to the concert, it may as well be the first time… See what I was saying about blowing things out of proportion? "When I saw that Rascal Flatts were playing at the Venetian, I couldn't resist."

An older couple from Houston joins the conversation, saying how much they enjoyed the concert as well. Mike's body freezes for a split second, registering that they have been listening to us. He glances my way, his brows furrowing. Flashing him my sweetest smile, I make small talk with them while he remains guarded. Soon, we wish them a good night when the elevator stops at their floor.

The second the suite door closes behind me, Mike stops in the middle of the entryway, shrugs, and explains his earlier reaction. "I expected them to look at us the wrong way. Maybe they didn't pay attention to how much my eyes were undressing you!"

"Oh, trust me, nobody missed that." My hips push him into the corner next to the bathroom door. Before he protests, I clasp his wrists and scatter kisses on his exposed collarbone. Damn, this man is addictive! And he's all mine. "Some people will care. Some people will hate. Some people won't. And for the record, judgmental people come in all shapes and sizes. Why should they be less open-minded because they're old enough to be our grandparents?"

"I guess." He writhes under my wicked mouth. "Looks like I'm the judgmental one today." Incapable of breaking free, he whimpers, speaking straight to my starved stiffy.

Pace yourself, big boy. You have more in store for him, remember?

I make an effort to concentrate on the conversation for now.

"I'm being ridiculous, aren't I?"

Before my need to fuck him overwhelms my last shred of common sense, I release him. Making a face, I raise my thumb and index finger, barely any space between them, in front of his face. "Just a tad bit." I wink. At least, he caught himself this time.

He's so ready.

Holding his hand, I lead him to the second bedroom, where a king-size bed is waiting for us.

"That's not where—"

My hand twirls him to face me and pulls his body flush with mine with a growl. My mouth crashes into his for an urgent kiss, his hand caressing my scalp. My groin gets the message and rubs against his, our pulses thundering in unison.

Reluctantly, I wrench my lips from his and cup his rosy cheeks as we cross the threshold. "You have no idea how much I'm enjoying my twenty-fifth birthday gift. And I'm sorry that you had to endure the concert. I loved it, but I know you hate country music!"

"But I don't hate you, Troy Hunter... Not anymore!" We snort at that, and he swats my ass, making me jump in surprise. He's right. So much has changed between us. In so little time. In so many ways. "And honestly, the concert was good. Best part was watching you have a great time, though. Now, I wanna return the favor... if you'll let me."

At first, his body shivers and his plump lips form a perfect O. Of course, my mind drifts to the gutter, imagining my dick sliding in and out of them. Warmth flares along the back of my neck, and I heave a pained sigh, controlling my need for him. I lean in and kiss the spot next to his earlobe, then look into his beautiful green eyes that are loaded with desire, expectation, and nervousness.

"Do you trust me?"

"Yes, Troy. I trust you."

I suggest getting clean before getting dirty, hoping that the hot water in the adjacent walk-in shower will ease some of his obvious apprehension that is completely natural. He obliges and we make quick work of stripping one another. There are lips. There are teeth. There are fingers.

The glass door is fogged with condensation, enveloping us in an out-of-time moment. Facing his back again, my heart hammers and I kneel. "I'll make it good for you, okay?"

With my breath on his toned ass, he fidgets and his head swivels to look at me. "Fuck, Troy! Stop teasing me and do whatever you want with me." His frustrated tone is endearing. "I'm dying here." Licking his lips, he splays his hands on the shower wall and widens his stance, as if guessing what's to come.

Incapable of keeping my unspoken promise, I nod none-theless, then tease his crease with the side of my wet pointer finger. Biting his lips, he stares, mesmerized. His ass cheeks alternatively clench and relax with each stroke, until they settle on the latter. Breaking eye contact to focus on the task at hand, I ignore my swelling hard-on, part his cheeks, and rustle up a grunt. Who cares if the water doesn't warm my skin? It's set ablaze when the tip of my greedy tongue probes for entry. Arousal hums in my blood when his body instantly relaxes, allowing my playful tongue to explore, swirl, and pleasure.

In a matter of minutes, his balance shifts, and I realize from the boisterous moaning that his right hand left the wall to jack himself off in sync with my efforts. Spellbound, I cease my TLC to watch him.

He tenses and his lustful eyes shoot daggers. When we first met, I couldn't have dreamed that this would happen. "Don't you dare stop!" Mike's voice is strained.

"Sorry, I got distracted," I say, smiling brightly, then work him over with one finger before my tongue resumes until his knees wobble.

This time, he tenses for an entirely different reason, so I intensify my rhythm and watch his shoulders ripple. He huffs and puffs, growls out my name, and comes in erratic spurts. I'll never get tired of bringing this man over the edge. Right after, he takes care of me and round two of scrubbing ensues, in between sloppy kisses, bad jokes, and dirty talk. His oversensitive skin shivers under my touch.

"You're driving me crazy, Hunter."

I chuckle at that, kneading his ass. "You ain't seen nothing yet, Clayton. Come on! Let me get you dry before you get wet for me… again."

Amused, I watch the naked man pull down the covers, snatch two pillows to place under his head, and lie sunny-side up on the mattress in two seconds flat. He takes one pillow from behind his head, sliding it under the small of his back, and, knees bent, spreads his legs as wide as possible so that I have the perfect view of what he's offering. This man is going to be the death of me!

"May I ask what triggered this?"

He takes short gulps of air. "Are you fucking kidding me?" His complaint prompts a salacious grin on his face, awakening my flaccid length. "You've been rimming my ass for the last half hour." His chest expands erratically as he catches his breath. "Finish the job, Hunter! Make me come... again." His hand gestures to show me where he wants me.

One hand on my waist, I take him in and lick my lips. "Bossy much?"

"Seriously?" He wiggles on the mattress, spreading his legs wider. He's magnificent.

My heart somersaults as I attempt to make sense of the extent of my desire for Mike Clayton. "Good thing I packed condoms and lube, then!" I wink, approaching him with a growing hunger and matching hard-on. "Top left drawer."

He twists his upper body to get what we need and throws everything next to him on the bed.

"It may not look like it, but I hadn't planned this, you know. We're not even gonna discuss who tops—"

"Come on, Troy." Glee. Irritation. Excitement. "It's pretty self-explanatory! Right now, that's how I want you." Mike, the mind-reader! "This is what got me off when I watched that porn I texted you about." He snatches the lube, pops the lid, and dribbles a reasonable amount on his middle finger. Then the needy man grins, rubs his semi, and starts fingering himself.

Frozen in place, I cock my head and gulp the lump that's lodged in my throat. "You're not playing fair."

His devilish laughter says it all... Well, almost, since he pants, "I want to watch your fingers stretch me until I scream for more. I want to watch your thick erection slide past the ring of muscle and against my prostate until I see stars. I want to watch you pound into me until I welcome the burn."

I sprint to the bed, roll down the condom, and lube up; my current state might limit the tenderness I intended for his first time. I scoot closer, between his legs, and position him so that I have easy access to his crease. Then, I follow his instructions to the letter. Eventually, my dick replaces his finger and my hand on his stiffy replaces his. His intoxicating scent makes my head spin.

It's obvious that I've hit the jackpot when his eyes roll back in his head. He growls. "Troy, oh, fuck..." He hisses. "More...." He moans. "Move faster!" Within seconds, he locks his ankles behind me, pulling me closer with each thrust. His command tears me out of my trance.

Soon enough, we're a hot mess. Covered in sweat. Aching muscles. Raw expletives. At once, a knot of pleasure coils where all my blood has pooled. My grip on him tightens and he claws at the sheet when his orgasm shoots through him. Next, my thigh muscles tremble as I plunge into him. Climax shoots through me, and I spill my pleasure into the condom, buried to the hilt one last time.

"Cuddle whore," I tease a moment later. Our spent bodies intertwined, I thread my fingers through his hair.

"Who would have thought?" He proudly grins, then his expression changes. "You know you're not a phase, right?" A sweet kiss lands on my forehead.

Although I avert his gaze, concealing my emotions is useless. I mouth a silent thank you, collecting my thoughts before looking him in the eye. This wonderful man brings out the best in me. I can't make promises, but there's no need. We're good together. "I love what we have, Mike." Somehow guessing that I'm not quite finished, he nods. I'll confess my life story tomorrow, but for now, there's one thing I have to say out loud.

"Our relationship."

CHAPTER 21
MY GUY

Mike

A s soon as the waiter from the cozy but noisy Meatball Shop in Chelsea sets Matteo's appetizing eggplant sandwich in front of him, he gets to work, licking the sauce from his lips with appreciative noises. Mundane conversation unfolds. His prominent New York job. My mom's long-term stay at my place. Our happy memories from way back when. His overly talkative mood confirms that he's waiting for the right moment to broach *the* subject. Since Ella dumped me, I kept test-driving women to find a suitable replacement. After Troy kissed me, I kept adding meaningless notches to my bedpost in the hope that they'd clear up my confusion. Now, things have changed; I avoided the truth until I was willing to welcome Troy into my life. Who needs a replacement when you meet that special someone, right?

Wow, I'm such a goner for Troy Hunter!

He downs what's left of his wine, then scrutinizes me with an arched brow. "So, how was Vegas, man?"

"Pretty cool. I went a little overboard, but it was so worth it." My fork snatches two meatballs out of the twenty in the aptly named Bucket O' Balls. Needless to say, Matteo couldn't help but sneer at my choice. Why is my craving for balls a novelty to him? "Thanks for your recommendation on the suite."

"It was a joke, moron! You guys didn't need three bedrooms."

"*Au contraire, mon ami!*" I wiggle my eyebrows. "We enjoyed the pool and didn't leave the suite... aside from the night of the concert."

Matteo helped me plan Troy's birthday surprise, but we have some catching up to do. Luckily, an opportunity presented itself thanks to Luana's girls' night out and Troy's gig in Portland, Oregon. In truth, I miss him like crazy; we spent so much time together recently that my arms are empty without him to hug. As for my mouth...

I debate on where to place the TMI-meter. There was a time when Matteo and I had no shame. We were two horny teenagers eager to score some easy pussies. But that was then. Giving some thought on what to say next, I cheat, stalling, and break eye contact while examining the contents of my large bucket.

Every time my mouth welcomes another ball, my stupid friend's gaze betrays his barely hidden amusement as he bites into his sandwich.

"What?" I ask with my mouth half-full. I swallow and inquire, "Do I have something on my face?" As much as I enjoy playing this game, I guess I'm having as much fun as he is. When I ordered my dinner, I knew my choice would lead to my friend being a smartass. Oddly enough, I'm not annoyed in the least that we're discussing my "new" sex life. I mean, we're guys and we're no longer single, so no more details in profusion, which is for the best.

Next week's massive Halloween party at Matteo's place, where I'll proudly introduce the hottest DJ on the planet as my boyfriend, will be a whole other story. At the thought, my heart soars.

"And?" His eyes narrow as he chews on his food. "Stop skirting the subject, Mike. I don't know what you're afraid of. You did the exact same thing the first time around. I'm on your side, remember? So, let me repeat the question: And?"

"Such a simple question." Again, I buy myself some time, one ball at a time, my eyes boring into his. "Such a meaningful question. Such a loaded question…"

"Nah! What happens in Vegas, stays in Vegas. But I'll welcome your confession." He winks. "Sex. Relationship. Future… The whole shebang. You know it's my duty as your best friend to make sure that you're okay, whether you're banging a chick or a dude. But come on, it has to be… different. So… where do you and Troy stand?"

"I know and I appreciate it. I'm fucking with you is all." I start counting on my fingers. "First, the sex is amazing, and that's all you'll get from me. Seriously, though… For the longest time, I envied your chemistry with your Brazilian beauty." I scratch my neck at my admission. "I finally found it with some-one… who happens to be a man. Second, Mr. Anti-commitment acknowledged our 'relationship status,' sharing that he's been exclusive for months and didn't tell me! Third, we don't speak about the future... It's too much, too soon. What matters is we're comfortable together. His nightlife activities are less time-consuming lately, and that's why I've been MIA."

He puts his fork down and gestures to dismiss my lingering guilt. "I couldn't be happier for you, Mike." He pats my bicep and refills my glass with pinot noir. "Has Eileen met Troy?" He considers my mom a friend, hence the first-name basis, but addresses my dad by his last name as I do with the Moretti elders.

Shaking my head, I explain that coming out to her was easier than planned. Her wild guess knocked the wind out of me. Apparently, a slight shift in my demeanor ignited her inquisitive mind. "She says I'm appeased..." I chug my wine as Matteo nods approvingly. "What gave me away, though, is that I stopped disclosing details of my *love life* like I used to." Granted, calling it that is a stretch, but my openness with my mom has boundaries. "Asking how it felt to be in love confirmed her assumption. Honestly, she's the best! It took me a while to register that her answers weren't gender-specific. Regardless, I want to wait a little before introducing him to my mom. Troy and I aren't into PDA, but we're not hiding either. I've convinced myself that I don't care about other people's reactions, but that's not entirely true. No one's called me a faggot to my face yet."

"Might never happen."

"I'm sure it eventually will, and I'm hoping my skin will be thicker by then. Also, I don't want to push him. Meeting my mom would make things somewhat official." I provide highlights of Troy's family debacle. "For now, it's too good to deny, and he's been so patient with me. I don't want to force him."

"You'll know when the time is right. Why don't we start with a double date? That is, if I can look past the stardom and see him as your boyfriend."

"About that… On the flight back from our sex marathon, he mentioned in passing that he knows his DJ success won't last and isn't a stable career choice, especially with all of the travel."

"What's wrong with wanting financial stability? Not everyone works for fun like us!" I open my mouth to counter his argument. I don't work for "fun," but I know what he means. He and I are fortunate enough that we can pursue our passions without worrying about making ends meet, thanks to a hefty trust fund.

"I already told you he works at a bar part-time, right?" Matteo nods, then he reads my mind and orders two coffees. "Out of nowhere, I learn that he's been scouting locations to invest in a bar and put his management skills to better use. I didn't want to pry because it doesn't concern me, but—"

"Whoa!" He holds his index finger in front of my face. "I beg to differ. You said it yourself, you guys are in a relationship."

"If I'm honest, the fact that he didn't ask for my opinion or say anything earlier bothers me."

"Speak up, Mike. That's how relationships work." Flagging down the waiter to request the check, he sips on his coffee, which gives me a minute to ponder that thought.

"You're right. It needs some fine-tuning, but I'm all over the place too. For some reason, I want to come out to my father before my mom sees Troy." A crease forming between my brows, I shrug noncommittally. Deep down, I'm irked by my own decision process. No matter how hard I fight it, his opinion matters to me. "I'm sure he won't be as supportive as my mom, yet the masochist part of me is compelled to tell him in person."

Braving the freezing wind whipping around us as we leave the restaurant, we agree to head back to my place.

"Can't your mom go with you?"

"Terrible idea! My mom's second marriage is falling apart. That's why she needed a break and came here with all sorts of bullshit excuses. My manipulative father is a master at reading people. I can't put her through that." His expression turns apologetic. "That's okay, though. I'm spending more time at Troy's. As for my mom, she'll be better off without Christopher. She has the worst taste in men!"

"Thank God you're breaking the cycle in that department."

"Words of wisdom."

I grin at him and his reply first comes in the form of a wink at my matter-of-fact comment. Then, he can't help but add a playful conclusion.

"Of course!"

CHAPTER 22
LATE NIGHT

Troy

Coming down from my high, I untie and kick off my Dr. Martens in haste as the door of my hotel room slams behind me.

Oops!

When I got ready hours ago, I debated on putting cowboy boots on for this gig, but Portland, Oregon's frigid October weather didn't give me much of a choice. As long as I sport my signature hat, nobody could care less about Monster Hunter's shoes. I shiver.

Exhaustion creeps in, and I strip down to my boxer briefs before heading to the bathroom to brush my teeth with a single idea in mind: hitting the sack. The quivering doesn't subside, and my head bops to bits and pieces of tonight's mix that buzz inside my head. Looking at myself in the bathroom mirror, the evidence of my sleep deprivation is clear. I don't mind the dark circles under my eyes; they're part of the life I chose.

Meandering to close the curtains, I mindlessly stare at the full moon that casts a faint glow. I make a wish, then remember that the moon isn't a shooting star and shrug at my own stupidity, knowing that it's time for me to call it quits. Head still tilting from side to side to the nonexistent rhythm, I automatically swivel to set my phone on the nightstand. Monster Hunter needs to vacate my body so that I can catch up on my beauty sleep. Although most people wake up to go to work at this indecent hour, I pine for recovery time. Shifting my weight from one foot to the other, I stare longingly at the inviting bed, then fall into it and slide under the covers.

I love the feeling of fresh sheets. Stretching my aching muscles that resulted from countless hours spent standing while mixing, I realize that I forgot to set my alarm. Reluctantly, I extend my arm, blindly reaching for said phone.

My initial reluctance turns to amusement when I notice a text from Mike. Maybe the full moon does grant wishes after all.

> *Mike: This or that? Pick one.*
> *This: phone call now. That: video call now. Miss ya.*

Mike sent it three hours ago, which would have given us ample time to talk before he had to leave for work.

My tired brain does the math to figure out his potential whereabouts, considering that it's already past nine in New York.

Troy: I pick YOU. Any way I can have you works for me. Sorry 4 the late reply. Just got back.

My fingers can't type fast enough. Though the sound of his velvety voice is a major turn-on, texting is a safer bet than calling.

Troy: Awesome & exhausting gig. My muscles are sore from standing/entertaining the guests. Miss U so bad. Let's catch up later.

My phone vibrates four times before my tired brain grasps that there's an incoming call.

"Later." One word from Mike, and my dick stirs to life, getting harder with every breath I take. My right hand grips my package over the fabric of my underwear and squeezes. The unbearable distance is killing me softly. On autopilot, I stifle a pained sigh once I'm comfortable. "Even miles away, I can hear your longing, baby." How has he become so acutely attuned to me in so little time? Another loud sigh ensues, and I swallow the aforementioned longing the best I can. Another rush of heat courses through my body, and I'm on fire in no time. Another firm squeeze only whets my appetite. This man…

"I… miss you so fucking bad." My voice comes out strangled. I don't even care that I'm wearing my emotions on my sleeve, although I'm shirtless. The Vegas trip definitely marked a turning point in our relationship. I acknowledged that we are a couple. He acknowledged that intimacy with a man doesn't scare him. We acknowledged that the line between love and hate is thinner than we originally thought. Well, I'm not sure where he stands as far as love is concerned; I know I'm far from ready to say the words, but who needs words when it's this good anyway?

While sipping on his morning coffee, he updates me on his late start, assuring me that talking to me is more important for now; and just like that, my grogginess dissipates. "I miss your face."

Since when have we expressed such desperation? "Not to be rude, but to be honest, it's not your face I miss the most."

"Oh, really? Didn't you say you were haunted by my cowboy hat?"

"I did." He chuckles, and right after, his tone turns businesslike and rushed. "Listen, I'm gonna have to call you back in a sec. I didn't think this through."

And with that, the fucker hangs up on me. No warning. No explanation. No goodbye. I drop my phone next to me. Equally annoyed and aroused, I spit into my palm, and my fingers find their way inside my boxer briefs to circle my girth. My pulse accelerates in anticipation. I work myself hard and fast. My shallow breathing stops when I'm interrupted by an incoming call. Caught in the act, I nonetheless press the green button with my other hand and put it on speaker.

"You're jacking off, aren't you?" *Busted!* Mike's tone is sulkier than a minute ago. I grunt in reply. "Let me see." His suggestion makes my skin tingle all over.

"Wh-What?" My thumb caresses my length a tad too harshly, then rubs its leaking tip. It sends the right kind of sensations, but I need more. I'm conflicted whether to dismiss his instruction and opt for a quick and messy release or to make it last longer and comply with something we've never done. Not that I have with anyone else, but I've come to learn that Mike's pleasure is often tied to a visual. My lover definitely watches too much porn!

"Oh, *please*." Damn, no matter how he says the word, needy or bossy, it arouses me to no end. "You're not playing fair and you know it."

"But it's so much more fun, don't you think?" I tease as the tip of my tongue traces the contour of my lips. "I'm not sure I'm ready for what you're asking anyway."

His bossy side finally takes over. "Don't play shy with me now, you little tease."

Ignoring his uncharacteristic remark and name calling, I snatch my phone with my free hand, move it closer to my ear, and focus on the random noises on the other end. "What are you doing?"

"What does it sound like I'm doing? I'm holding the phone between my left shoulder and cheek while getting naked for you, asshole! Thank goodness I'm working from home today! I had to hurry back upstairs because my throbbing cock needed some TLC, and I started stroking it in the middle of my kitchen. Then, it dawned on me that my mom could barge in at any time. That's why I hung up on you." Mike's confession sinks in as I continue my ministrations, wondering if I'll find my voice, but he doesn't give me the opportunity. "Now, do as I say and let me see. I'll gladly return the favor."

His ardor baffles me. This is a full 180 degrees from the time that Mike texted and basically friend-zoned me while I was in LA... right before he surprised me by picking me up at the airport. Who would have thought we'd come such a long way in so little time after our awkward start?

"Once upon a time, you'd have said 'please, Troy.'"

"I already did, and I'm afraid I'm past begging, *Sir*." I don't miss his sarcasm. "Quit skirting my request."

"Request? It sounds more like a command to me."

"Troy!" His warning's more like a growl between gritted teeth.

Without further ado, I get rid of my superfluous piece of clothing and put him out of his misery. As soon as I prop the phone against the comforter and switch on my camera, I lick my lips at the breathtaking view.

"Perfect angle, baby." I'm not sure where he put his phone to make this work, but I'm granted with a clear visual of his half-mast gaze and engorged erection. My mouth waters.

"I figured you'd like it." With his free hand, he aims for his balls, torturing me with this enticing visual. The erotic little noises he makes amplify my lust every time his chiseled chest heaves up and down.

"I so wish I was there to lick every inch of your skin." I bite the inside of my cheeks to avoid chuckling at the sound he makes when I widen my stance. My fist travels up and down my shaft.

"That's it, baby. Pinch your balls for me... *please*." Again, his sarcastic tone isn't lost on me, but I'm too far gone to call him out on it. I oblige and am rewarded with the filthiest sound that I've ever heard. I shiver, registering how close I am. I want more. It's time to see if his bravery has limits.

"Happy with your own porn clip?"

"I... can't... complain." Catching his breath, I revel in his flushed cheeks. From the way his eyes drift away, I know he's almost ready too.

"What do you say we add a little ass play to the mix?"

I hear no complaint. Instead, an eager and always prepared Mike reaches for the lube. He then positions his muscular body to the side so that I don't miss the action when his coated middle finger toys with his crease before it disappears inside of him. My eyes widen at the view and intoxicating sounds escaping his mouth that tell me that he's undoubtedly hit his prostate.

Biting the corner of my mouth, I ask in a hot whisper, with my heart thumping, "Do you have any idea how fucking hot you are, Mike?" Shortly after, I follow his lead without waiting for his answer. My ravenous body writhes under my touch and decides it needs two digits; it's a good thing I always have a packet of lube in my wallet that's within reach on the nightstand. With both hands working to get myself off, I'm nonetheless acutely aware of the kinky voyeur. Our eyes lock at regular intervals while getting high on the show we're putting on for each other. Squeeze. Release. Push. Pull. In. Out. And repeat relentlessly.

"Right back at you, Troy Hunter." When my name rolls off of his tongue like an X-rated promise, I squirt all over my hand and lower stomach as I let his name out in a blissed-out cry. "Fuck... I've never seen anything... anyone... this hot. Ever."

Soon enough, my eyes are glued to the screen as I witness his elbow fly to cover his mouth to muffle the desperate groans of his release. His beautiful body tenses. His sweaty face reddens. His appetizing cock shoots his pleasure across his own skin instead of mine.

Panting and sleepy, I whisper a thank you. "No one's hotter

than you, Mike Clayton. I can't wait for our reunion. I can't wait to touch you the way you touched yourself. I can't wait..." My body is both heavy and weightless. My voice is both edgy and sluggish. My heart is both racing and full. I'm already drifting to sleep.

"Me neither."

CHAPTER 23
HERE COMES THE SHOCK

Mike

Bundled in my dark green winter North Face parka, black scarf, and matching beanie, I shiver on Troy's doorstep.
"Hey, baby, I couldn't take it anymore." I shouldn't have raised my voice, but it slipped out before I could stop myself.

What was I thinking? Grumbling at my thoughtlessness, I prick up my ears and, once I'm certain the place is peaceful, close the door behind me, as gently as my excitement allows.

For the first time, I used the key that Troy gave me when I impulsively told my mom to stay as long as she needed. My perfect boyfriend figured that I might want to crash without permission. His one-bedroom apartment in Park Slope is a typical bachelor pad, small but homey with minimalist décor. It's right off Prospect Park, the Central Park of Brooklyn, which makes it a trendy neighborhood, in a good way. The single draw-back is having to hike all the way to Manhattan for work after I sleep over! Maybe I should convince my mom to check into a hotel after all…

Missing Troy like crazy, I tossed and turned all night long.

To shake off my exhaustion, I spent ample time swimming at the local gym at the crack of dawn to avoid awaking my mother who's sleeping above my own gym. Then, I sprinted here on autopilot, acknowledging that I'd been sporting a semi at the mere thought of him.

"You have no idea what I'm up to," I murmur to myself, pretending to address my lover that I'll surprise by sliding into his warm bed stark naked… after I fix breakfast so that it's ready when I'm done blowing him.

This week's been so hectic that we only saw each other twice. Seventy-six hours without his warm body is an eternity. I yearn for a skin-on-skin contact. Vegas unleashed my horny side and we've been fucking like rabbits since then... Or rather, he's been fucking me. Returning the favor is next on my list, although I'm torn between the urge to claim his glorious ass and the hesitation that I won't fit in his tight hole. My face flames with these memories in mind as I deposit the box of goodies from Buttermilk Bakeshop on the counter of his open-plan kitchen, then rub my cold hands together.

A content sigh leaves my mouth as I shed my leather gloves and the rest of my winter gear, placing everything on a barstool shortly after. My chest swells with pride at my uncharacteristically bold move.

Striding to the fridge, I grab the ground coffee and fix a large pot; we're both heavy coffee drinkers. I inhale deeply, letting the aroma fill the room and my nostrils. That's one of my favorite scents, apart from Troy's skin, of course. A wry smile on my face, I glance at Troy's bedroom door and get undressed, holding my breath in a ridiculous attempt to remain unnoticed. Butterflies swarm in my stomach when I imagine my sleepy, sexy, and very naked lover. Later today, we'll be celebrating Halloween with our friends, including his partners in crime, Claire and Drake, who I have yet to meet.

But right now, as I sneak into Troy's dark room, clad in only my boxer briefs that he'll be too happy to get rid of himself, I have one thing on my mind and the perfect line for it: "I don't want to do anything but you."

Tugging my throbbing cock, I squint to adjust to the darkness. His bedroom's immense, compared to the rest of the place; it's where he stores his DJ equipment and other music stuff, whose names I keep forgetting.

Quietly, I turn towards the bed, guided by my irrepressible need and his light snores. My heart skips a beat. My throat constricts. My legs give way. Transfixed, I swallow the bitter taste of Troy's betrayal as I spy the man I love in bed with a woman whose face is hidden by a mane of dark curls.

Son of a bitch! My hand releases my manhood that didn't get the memo yet. It takes an eternity to tear my eyes from this disgusting sight. I could wake them both and make a scene, but my need to throw up is stronger. Instead, I sprint from the room, fetch my clothes that I put back on in haste, and grab the pastry box to erase the evidence of my visit.

Quietly closing the door on what could have been my future, I pause at the threshold. My heart sinks as I let the tears well like the crushed, hopeful, and weak soul that I am.

You know what, Troy Hunter? I break from my thoughts and voice my hurt.

"Fuck you!"

———

THIRTY-FIVE MINUTES OF WEIGHT LIFTING. Forty-five minutes of lower body exercises. An hour on the treadmill... and it's still not enough to calm my frayed nerves. Blindly swiping the beads of sweat collecting on my forehead, I don't stop. I can't stop. I won't stop.

Observing myself in the full-wall mirrors isn't an option today. I don't need to be reminded that I'm a flustered mess. So, instead, I've opted to keep my eyes closed for the majority of my workout.

Noise-cancelling earbuds in, I lip sync the lyrics to the music blasting in my ears. The rest of the world ceased to exist long ago. There's just me and the growing self-hatred. No matter how heavy I go on the free weights, my overthinking mind is on a roll. My stupid heart sinks. My useless body is leaden.

How could I have been so gullible? How could the piece of shit betray me like this? How could I let this pseudo-affair go on for so long?

At once, the treadmill slams to a complete stop, and I pop my eyes open and grip the handle right before tumbling from the equipment. I'm brought back to a reality that I'm not ready to face just yet.

What the hell?

It takes me a second to register that the music's volume prevents me from holding a conversation. Palming my earbuds, I look at my surroundings, trying to catch my breath before the weight of angry eyes meets my own.

"What do you think you're doing?"

"Huh?"

"I said, what do you think you're doing?"

"What does it look like I'm doing, Mom?" My tone is less than polite, but I can barely breathe, and anyway, she deserves it for interrupting my escape. Blinking the sweat from my eyes, I take in the form of my mother. Standing on the other side of the treadmill, she's wearing a purple robe that remains tightly closed under her crossed arms.

"Don't use that tone with me, Michael. I'm warning you, I'm two seconds away from using your full name!" Her voice is even, but I don't miss the lingering threat. It magically puts a halt to my pity party.

"I'm sorry, Mom." Still huffing and puffing, I snatch the hem of my T-shirt to wipe away the sweat dripping down my back. I wish I could get rid of the stench as well, but that'll have to wait. Only now do I realize that I should have headed to the gym instead of working out here. Of course, I pissed her off! How could I be so forgetful and thoughtless?

"Do you care to share why you couldn't wait until a reasonable hour? I mean, I heard you loud and clear from upstairs. What prompted your sudden urge to work out like a man possessed?"

"I needed to unwind." I grumble. Without preamble, I wrench out of my soaked shirt. "Now, if you'll excuse me"—I swivel towards the small bathroom behind me—"a shower is next on my list."

"Stop right there!" Her command is delivered a notch higher than necessary but has the desired effect. I turn to face her again, fingers combing through my wet hair. "Does it have something to do with Troy?"

Hearing his name rolling off of her tongue for the first time warms my heart for a split second... until I snap out of my trance and remember. The hope. The hurt. The betrayal. Averting her piercing eyes, I shrug, helpless. My hands land in my shorts pockets and I stare at her, my breathing returning to normal, although my chest aches for an entirely different reason.

You played me. You used me. You lied to me.

I should grab my water bottle, but I can't escape my mom's eyes. Confusion. Sadness. Hurt.

"What changed between the moment I went to bed last night and now?"

Mmm... good one!

How can I convey what I witnessed? The moment that crushed my perfect dream.

Yeah, it was all a dream, you stupid fuck!

I shake my head in disbelief. Still, I can't stop from blurting out the only word that encompasses my current state.

"Everything."

CHAPTER 24
BROKEN HALOS

Troy

"Here." I pass a plate laden with a bagel and lox over the counter to Anna, then turn my back to her, pouring coffee into two mugs and slipping onto the barstool beside her.

Warmth invades my cheeks as I offer her a half-smile, then worry my lip when Mike's naked body flashes through my dirty mind, betraying my constant yearning for my boyfriend. My heart swells at that.

My boyfriend! And to think that Mike was anxious because I was his first… Why didn't I tell him that he's my first in so many ways, too? I plan to rectify that when we meet up later today. Hopefully before Matteo's Halloween party, but we haven't made definitive plans yet. Grabbing my iPhone from the counter, I shoot him a quick text.

Anna rubs her face with her palms, then attacks her breakfast. "Thanks." Her puffy eyes match the dark circles under mine due to my hangover.

"I'm sorry that Nick cheated on you, Anna. He sounded like a decent guy."

My Dutch friend's eyes are glassy, and I immediately regret bringing up the subject. "He's a piece of shit!" The fact that she heard about it through the grapevine was the icing on the rotten cake. "I thought he wanted something steady." She shrugs. "Stupid me! He's a famous photographer and can have any woman he wants."

"Don't even go there. It has nothing to do with you, okay."

Anna kisses my forehead. Out of reflex, I check my messages and my brows knit. I sigh, noticing that Mike didn't read my text, although it's already past 10:00 a.m., which isn't like him. He's a light sleeper, even on weekends. Chasing the lingering annoyance, I convince myself that he's still asleep and turn my attention back to Anna. Last night's goals were damage control and being there for my best friend... which made me forget to text Mike goodnight; he can't be pissed because of that, right?

My long road to self-awareness, relationship material, and allowing myself to envision a future with someone is this morning's hot topic, thanks to her never-ending line of questioning. I fidget. I blush. I cough.

Damn, her scrutiny makes me squirm!

"By the way, thank you for letting me crash at your place, borrow a T, and holding my hair when my stomach rebelled. I was so engrossed in my pity party that I didn't say the words."

"Anytime. You're always welcome to stay here. What are friends for, right?" I wink. "I drank way more than my limit as well. Cocktails are traitorous! It's a miracle I don't have a headache."

"Also, thanks for hugging me as I fell asleep. I desperately needed it."

"Like I said, what are friends for? You're the sister that I never had." I frown at my own statement. Who needs a blood line when Anna is the perfect surrogate sister? A much better fit than friends with benefits... And just like that, she reads my mind.

"You're my best friend, Troy. Who would have thought we would suck at the benefit part?"

"Well, I have plenty of benefits sucking someone else, thank you very much." I stick my tongue out and we snicker.

With Anna in the shower, I clean up and do the dishes, thoughtful. I mull over Mike's silence while texting with Claire, who's tagging along with Drake tonight, courtesy of Matteo. "The more, the merrier," he replied when Mike suggested it last week.

Before I know it, a dolled-up Anna appears in the living room, her baby blues edged with concern. "You okay, Troy? Your jaw is clenched so hard it's painful to watch." I grumble incoherent words. A brow spiked up, she's next to me in no time. "Speak up!"

"Mike's usually by his phone. He hasn't messaged me yet. I don't know... Something's wrong." I shake my head dismissively and pour myself another cup of coffee. "Anyway, I forgot to tell you that I'm DJing at tonight's party. Wanna tag along?" A couple of texts later, it's settled, and Matteo inquires whether Mike and I will wear matching costumes. I gulp my escalating worry and elude the question, then end the exchange.

Instead, I jut my chin in Anna's direction, wordlessly offering her more coffee, and fill her mug. "Thanks for making coffee this morning, by the way." We clink our mugs and chuckle. "I'm glad you found my stash. I don't know if I was in any shape to make it myself!" I force out a laugh.

"I didn't make coffee." Her confused eyes narrow. "The pot was full when I woke up. I thought you set a timer..."

That's when my body connects with reality. And freezes. When my brain connects the dots. And short-circuits. When my eyes connect with their surroundings. And widen.

A black leather glove is discarded by the front door. Mike's. My heart skips a beat. Of all the mornings Mike could have stopped by, he chose today. My mouth is parched. Dread courses down my spine as I imagine what he saw and felt. My blood runs cold.

Snatching my coat and wallet, I kiss Anna's forehead. "Sorry, I got to go." And slam the door in my wake, yelling, "Fuckity fuck fuck!"

FIVE AUDIO MESSAGES. Ten texts. Fifteen PMs on social media... I kept my communications clipped; we need to address this face-to-face. Why is my man giving me the silent treatment?

Mike doesn't trust me. Mike said he does, but doesn't. Mike doesn't love me... Wait! What? Holy shit! Did it have to come to this for me to realize that I didn't want to lose him? Am I in love with Mike?

My lungs burn. I rock back on my heels on the stoop of his 11th Street brownstone. Because I forgot my beanie in my haste and stubbornly refused to put my hood up, my damp hair sticks to my forehead and rivulets of water trickle down my face. I mentally curse the shitty Halloween weather and the nerve-racking subway ride.

Heart in my throat, I've been pondering my next move for the last half hour, in hopes that my favorite Manhattanite would emerge from his lair and listen to the voice of reason... aka mine. I need to make sure that he's okay, right? Make sure that I'm not imagining things, right? Make sure that he shares my feelings, right?

My fingers twitch in my coat pocket. "I'm not using his key." Tempting me, Mike's key burns like the Grail. "I'm not using his key." My new mantra is muttered between clenched teeth as I stand in front of his fucking door... which I haven't knocked on yet. Instead, I stare at my wet boots and shake beads of water from my hair.

"You must be Troy?" A warm feminine voice wrenches me from my inner turmoil. My heart lurches like I've been caught with my hand in the cookie jar.

Pretending that I'm not a sopping mess, I lift my head and find the kindest pair of eyes studying me. They belong to a regal-looking redhead. It's clear where Mike got his good looks from. Nodding at her assumption, I offer a sheepish smile. "May I come in? Although, I probably owe you an explanation first."

"Don't be silly! I apologize for my lack of manners. Please, come on in." She moves out of the way and gestures for me to enter. "I saw someone on the monitor and expected you to ring the doorbell! You're drenched; I had to put you out of your misery."

"You're my fairy godmother then?"

"Ohhh, you have no idea! Hurry, or you'll catch a cold."

I nod a silent thank you. *Why is she completely unfazed by my presence?* Hesitant to step in, I cough, guarded, as if expecting Mike to storm down the steps; the familiar entryway is suddenly intimidating.

The chatty woman carries on cheerfully, taking my coat rather than acknowledging the elephant in the foyer. "Michael's in serious need of comfort." She winces. "I'm not saying that to make you feel bad." Her kind words cleave my broken heart in two. I can't stand that Mike's miserable because of what he saw. Should I blame this clusterfuck on shitfaced Anna or on Mike's lack of trust in us? Granted, seeing a woman in my bed must have pissed him off big time... How could he believe that I'd betray him? Frustration rolls through me, sending annoying tingles across my skin. "What's going on between you and my boy is yours to sort out. I won't interfere."

Scratching my neck, I stare. She welcomed me, but I'd hate

for her to think I'm a jerk for messing with her son, in more ways than one. "Did he say anything?"

"Not really. He's been so excited about Matteo's party for days. So, when he growled that he wouldn't go, I knew something was up. He's so... angry." I catch my breath as her voice cracks. "I woke up this morning because he made such a ruckus working out. He punished his body for hours, like a man possessed. I know that Michael needs *you*," she declares. "I let you in because you wouldn't be here, soaked, if it weren't important to you. So, I'm going to run errands and give you guys some space, okay." She envelops me in the sweetest hug. I sigh when she releases me. "I would have preferred to meet you under better circumstances, but it's so nice to meet you. I hope I'll see you again soon, Troy."

Sucking in a breath, I take the stairs two at a time. I hear him groan from the landing. "I said I needed alone time, Mom." He must be under the comforter because he sounds muffled. I quiver, steeling myself for what lies ahead.

Tiptoeing into the room, I silently sidle up to him and stifle a laugh when I witness his body wrapped in blankets like a spring roll. The only visible part of him is the top of his hair.

"Leave me alone, Mom."

I bite the inside of my cheeks to stay incognito for a bit longer. Ignoring my damp clothes, I swiftly straddle his big body, rip the comforter from the bed, and grab his wrists. He doesn't have time to register who's on top today. I place them over his head and make a mental note to recreate this scene later. My dripping hair tickles his breathtaking but blank face.

"Get out of my sight, fucker!" His spite doesn't ruffle me. It's cute that he believes he can fight me, oblivious to the fact that I was once a real cowboy. He may be stronger, but I've wrangled bigger bulls than him. Yeah, size doesn't always matter!

Bending over his upper body, I whisper into his ear, "That's

Mister Fucker to you, baby." Despite the limited space, he shakes his head at the term of endearment. "I brought back the glove you left behind."

There!

His green eyes widen and he opens his plump mouth to speak. Once again, I'm faster; my tongue fills his mouth to remind him how good we are together. He's forced to open up for me, but resists anyway.

My entire body goes lax at his intoxicating taste. I'm home again. Our hearts beat so erratically, I'm afraid that they'll explode before he surrenders. My chest constricts with every hungry stroke. Reluctantly, I pry my mouth from his. "Thanks for fixing coffee this morning, baby."

"Get off of me, fucker!" His eyes are shooting daggers. I don't care. "We're done."

"Far from it." The tip of my tongue teases the side of his face. His head lashes from side to side, but he's stuck. "I know you think you know, but you don't." His gym shorts can't conceal his arousal that presses against mine. "Anna, my broken-hearted best friend, needed a shoulder to cry on. We drank way too much." My confession is met with grunts and expletives. "Sharing a bed with her used to include benefits." He grumbles. "It's over. I told you, I haven't slept with anyone else since we… kissed on the boat." He needs to hear this.

"Your secret best friend that's never come up? How convenient!"

"Oh, you know her; we owe her big time. Without her in Paris, there would be no us!"

His jaw drops. "Seriously?"

"Yup… You once said you trusted me. Now stop being so dramatic. I didn't mention that Anna's staying over, and I apologize. End of story. You and I are going to Matteo's party. I'll introduce you to my friends Anna, Claire, and Drake. *That*'s not up for discussion." His wrestling ceases. Scattering kisses along his neck, my face breaks into a grin when his stiffy grinds against mine. *Good boy!* "And for the record, remember that I'm a man of my word. Being exclusive means something." As soon as I release his wrists, his hands grope my ass, skimming my body along his. Lust floods from my head down to my toes. In a ragged breath, I add, "You hurt me because you didn't trust me. No matter what people like your father ingrained in you, Mike, you're perfect as you are. I wouldn't want you any other way. You are worth it… and I—" I pause, tongue-tied all of a sudden.

"You what?" His pupils dilate with need as they cage mine.

My words bubble up from my throat. My pulse thunders in my ears.

"Love you."

CHAPTER 25
ALL OF IT

Mike

"Hey, man, good to see you!" lanky Simon shouts over the live music that a certain cowboy is performing at the behest of his number one fan, Matteo Moretti.

Ever since our arrival, a few hours earlier than the other guests so that Troy could set up his equipment, my Italian friend has been trailing after my man like a well-trained puppy, rudely neglecting his other thirty guests. It's both endearing and pathetic, and I can't wrap my mind around his fascination with Troy's DJ performances. I'm way more interested in Troy's other skills, but happy to be the only one benefiting from them now that Anna-gate has been resolved.

A champagne flute in one hand, my British friend, who I haven't seen since Matteo's wedding, pats my back with the other.

"Good to see you, too. It's been a while. Where are Tweedledee and Tweedledum?" I ask when he releases me. I'm happy that my friends were able to take a week off from work so that they could come tonight.

"Ha-ha! Good one." His hearty laugh resonates in my ears. "They're always up to something." He fills me in on their latest shenanigans, then gulps what's left of his expensive champagne in one go. "Last time I saw them, they were dancing as close as possible to your celebrity friend."

Right, my celebrity friend!

That statement sends a shiver down my stiff spine. It's wrong on so many levels, and not the celebrity part. Well, after we kissed and made up for a couple of hours at my place, Troy declared that he'd made up his mind and wanted to settle down rather than pursue a dream career that will quickly fade. Wary that our relationship might be the impetus behind his sudden change of heart, I argued, and he countered that it was his own decision and had been contemplating it for months. He decided to invest his DJ profits in a bar and wants me to tag along the next time he visits the 8ᵗʰ Avenue location to get my feedback. Apparently, this is his idea of a compromise between his job interests—compromises neither of us is willing to make as far as our relationship goes. Either way, I was relieved that he asked for my opinion.

Anyway, I intend to correct the celebrity friend misconception... soon. As determined as I was to come out to our friends, Troy and I agreed that flaunting my supposedly new sexual orientation would be counter-productive. The point isn't to convince my friends to accept the "new me," rather to show them that I'm comfortable and happy with our relationship. A relationship that happens to be with a wonderful man who evokes a whirlwind of sensations in me. We're not here to make a statement, but to enjoy Matteo's party. We struggled to pick out costumes on the fly, but then, I rummaged through my drawers and serendipity happened... again.

Granted, I steer clear of the makeshift dance floor and keep my back to the DJ to avoid mauling him in front of his rapt audience. I'm not afraid, worried, or freaked out like I was at

Matteo's birthday party. As crazy as it sounds, Troy owned me from the moment I returned his revenge kiss at that club. One day, I'll tell him that if it hadn't been for one of my coworkers insisting that I join their celebration, I wouldn't have been there. Clubs aren't my thing and that's why I got sloshed. One day, I'll tell him how he haunted my Parisian dreams—him and his damn cowboy hat—and I was too chicken-shit to face the obvious, no matter how clairvoyant Lisa tried to open my eyes. One day...

That was then, this is now.

So, upon Simon's request, for the umpteenth time, I parrot an edited version of how Monster Troy and I got to talking on the cruise. Despite my distaste of techno, clubs and whatnot... Of course, some details remain private. Such as our raw, feral, insane chemistry.

Heading towards the bar to munch on some finger food and get a refill, he scolds me for the simple black Netflix T-shirt that I'm sporting. "What's the deal with your Halloween costume? It's not like you to slack on something like this." He goes on, reminding me of countless costume parties. "You didn't put in much effort tonight." He chortles, moving to a quieter corner to allow more room for the other guests.

My hip rests on the bar. "*Au contraire, mon ami.*" I wiggle my eyebrows. "Wasn't planned, but it worked out perfectly. It's been a while since matching costumes were so fitting." I bark out a laugh.

"Matching costumes?" Simon snatches a couple of pulled pork sliders, wolfs them down, and quirks an eyebrow, scanning the room. To tease him rather than provide more information, I ask who's playing Cleopatra to his Julius Caesar, and instead of offering a witty comeback, he smiles sheepishly. Wondering why, I get my answer when I notice who's approaching and smile at the familiar face.

"There you are, baby." Stella, my former hook-up in Brazil, who's dressed as Cleopatra, addresses Simon, her coveting glance revealing more than her words. She adjusts her black wig, then sips on her frou-frou cocktail.

I should have put two and two together when I saw Simon's costume! Feigning outrage, I gesture theatrically towards Caesar and exclaim, "Et tu, Brute?" although Caesar should be saying this, not me. Realizing that I'm not privy to their status, she looks from her boyfriend to me, and her angelic face gets flustered. I wink as he freezes. "Oh, come on, guys! Stella and I..." —I alternatively point between Stella and myself— "were never an item. Right?"

Relief flashes across their unnecessarily guilty faces. She shrugs and nods, sounding too eager to switch topics. "So, besides letting your hair grow, how have you been, Mike?"

I'm tempted to say, "gay... or bi," but I can't stand labels, not because I'm ashamed; I've merely decided to be myself. I'm tempted to say, "thoroughly fucked in the best of ways," but that might be too blunt. I'm tempted to say, "happily deep-throated by my sexy as hell boyfriend," but she probably doesn't care about that or how I'm working on my gag reflex. Yeah, I'm not here to brag, provoke, or broadcast.

So, I opt for another approach. "Busy with work. Happy in New York. Attached..." I trail off, pondering what to reveal, but Simon saves me the trouble.

"Oh, is that so?" His voice is tinged with mockery. "And yet, you didn't mention anything!" Thoughtful, he rubs his chin.

"Looks like we're even, then." I wink at the couple.

Stella giggles, wraps her arm around Caesar's waist, and tiptoes to peck his cheek. Stroking my forearm as encouragement, she taps her foot on the hardwood floor. "Spill the beans, Clayton."

"Let's see... *Simon says...*" I chortle as I air quote the words. *Asshole!* "I'm not wearing a costume, per se, but my significant other and I are wearing matching ones."

"Oh, right, matching non-costumes and the mysterious significant other!"

I smirk, wave over a waiter, and down the shot of vodka, enjoying the slight burn. Caught up in my own game, I will myself to conceal my growing irritation while part of me is getting a kick out of tormenting him. "Here's another hint: There's nothing 'mysterious' about my other half." Again, I air quote Simon's words.

He grumbles between clenched teeth. "Where did you guys meet then? Brown or blue eyes?" Wow, Simon's on a roll. "Blonde or not?"

"What is this? Twenty questions? I'm not answering any of this… or that!" The corner of my mouth quirks up at the mention of Troy's favorite game.

"Guys, relax, will you?" Stella admonishes. I'm not responsible for her man getting all worked up over nothing. "By costume, Mike, you meant lack of, right?" Her tone is amused.

Stunned that she doesn't pry for more, I scratch the back of my neck, wondering if it'll register...

"Great minds, Stella." Simon snorts and high-fives his girl.

"Ha-ha!" They don't miss my sarcastic tone. Sighing, I swivel my upper body towards the nearest bartender to order myself a second shot and more champagne for Simon. I drink, then turn my attention back to my friends.

"I told him the exact same thing minutes ago." He sneers, swats my forearm, and they clink glasses.

Torn whether to disclose the mystery before Troy's done with his set, I shamelessly redirect the conversation to our earlier topic, eager to hear how these two grew closer. That's how I learn that my early departure from Rio was profitable for all three of us.

"What are you guys talking about?" Scandinavian Magnus and British James ask in unison; the former has a possessive arm around a woman's shoulder. Must be his date since they're dressed as John Smith and Pocahontas. Why James chose to dress up as Beckham back when he was with the PSG is beyond me... considering that October in New York in fucking brutal!

"Relationships... Costumes... and Mike's denial on both accounts."

"Will you get off my dick already?" I grunt, glowering at his assumption. "I am *not* in denial. This *is* my fucking costume!" My thumb and index finger pinch the fabric and pull on it.

"Yeah!" James taps on Simon's forearm and looks my way. "I saw you talking to a hot girl with a T-shirt that could match yours, although I'm not exactly sure..." He halts as if trying to uncover a hidden meaning.

"You're referring to the tall brunette with amazing blue eyes, right?" He nods excitedly. "I'm glad you're more observant than this moron." I swat the back of Simon's head, letting him recover the sliding laurel wreath. Snickers follow. "Anna is all yours. She definitely doesn't want to be part of my sandwich!" It doesn't take a rocket scientist to guess where this is going. James's eyes shine with playfulness, and we fist bump like we did over a decade ago. "I'm not sharing anyway!"

As if on cue, the live music is replaced by familiar tunes with a Halloween vibe. My body hums with anticipation, although my eyes remain trained on my friends.

I feel him. I sense him. I smell him. Goosebumps spread across my skin, and I shiver. His essence enthralls my entire being and I nearly combust when his knuckles brush the small of my back. *What is this man doing to me?*

I tilt my head and meet Troy's hungry eyes. The air thickens, as does my semi. My heart skips a beat when he stands so close that I ache to touch him, but my antsy fingers refrain. Lust builds in my balls, my black pants suddenly too tight.

His entire demeanor is a mix of hyper from his performance and laid-back from the aftermath. He catches his breath as my best friend—portraying Steve Trevor *sans* Wonder Woman—

compliments the artist, along with Claire and Drake who are portraying the perfect couple that they aren't—Bonnie with purple dreadlocks and a heavily tattooed Clyde—while Anna is nowhere to be seen.

Staring at Troy's forest green T-shirt with a hashtagged word, Stella exclaims, "Great shirt, Mister DJ!" She gasps. "Thanks for the hints, Mike." She plants a quick kiss on my cheek. "Check it out!" She shakes Simon's arm and points her index finger my way. "Netflix." Then in Troy's direction. "Chill… Oh my God!" She puts her empty glass down on the bar to clap her hands together excitedly. "Netflix. Chill…" She pauses, giving our audience time to register the implications. "Awesome costume!" She peers sideways at Simon.

Sighing, I prefer to set things straight… so to speak! Like I felt the need to do the last time that my friend Lisa and I Face-Timed; to say that her unwavering support startled me is an understatement.

I address Stella and my friends, but only have eyes for Troy. "Guys, let me properly introduce you to Troy." I slip my hand into his. "The man that I love."

His face flushes and his eyes pop out of their sockets at my public declaration. Tightening his grip on my hand, his question comes out ragged. "You do?"

About to steal a toe-curling kiss from him, I realize that, sometimes, words do speak louder than actions. So I lean into him and whisper, grazing his earlobe,

"Definitely."

EPILOGUE - YOU & ME

Troy

A YEAR LATER

"Let's do this!" Resolve fills my brave man's voice as one of his hands palms the car key fob. Throughout the drive from Greenwich Village to Boston, he's been oscillating between apprehension and relief. The way his jaw ticked. The way his smile widened. The way his body stiffened...

"You know what?" My abrupt question stops him in his tracks. He turns my way, his penetrating gaze taking my breath away. I scratch the back of my head, then place my hands on my thighs to focus on the moment rather than my need to fuck him senseless. My craving for Mike Clayton isn't about to subside, but I've learned to behave in public places. "You probably should go in by yourself. Test the waters, you know."

His mouth parts, and I give him time to say his piece, but he remains muted. Instead, he kills the engine of his BMW. The cool atmosphere that Pearl Jam offers lingers; *Soldier of Love.* How fitting for today's reunion! We've learned to appreciate various genres. One step at a time. How we approach anything that happens to arise. Hand in hand. Like discriminatory insults and unsolicited comments from strangers. Head on. Like his dad's stroke that granted a new perspective for all of us, his father included.

"What?" His tone is suddenly clipped. His breathing falters, and I shiver as I notice the lines that appear on his forehead. His green eyes darken with what I decipher as anger. At once, the air shifts. *Damn, he really can get riled up over nothing!* "The whole point of this Boston trip was for my father to meet the person I love, for real. Because, as Harry Burns would say in my mother's favorite movie, *When Harry Met Sally*: 'I love that you get a little crinkle above your nose when you're looking at me like I'm nuts. I love that after I spend the day with you, I can still smell your perfume on my clothes. And I love that you are the last person I want to talk to before I go to sleep at night!'"

"I wear *cologne*, not perfume, and I don't get a crinkle above my—"

He grunts, gesturing for me to shut up. "That's not the point, Troy Hunter! Focus, God dammit!"

"Okay, okay! I get it, you love smelling my *perfume* because you're a creeper!" Feigning a joke so that he'll simmer down, I realize that I've failed miserably with his next words.

"I can't believe I forgot to tell my mom about quitting my designer job when we saw her yesterday. I know she'll support me as long as I'm happy, especially since we're building a life together, and I can always draw and design as a hobby. Plus, she knows that I don't take decisions like this lightly. I wish I remembered. Ugh. I'm sorry. I didn't mean to ramble." His fingers run through his unruly hair that's so soft to the touch, and I itch to reach for him. Luckily, he's too bogged down by his frustration to notice, but unfortunately continues his rant... This isn't how I'd envisioned this going! "I would've introduced you to my dad a year ago if it hadn't been for his sudden trip to the ER." He grips the wheel until his knuckles turn white.

"Baby, I know that." As I'm well aware of how Mr. Clayton's months of physical therapy took a toll on his son's mental health. Guilt. Remorse. Secrets. "This year hasn't exactly been a walk in the park and put a lot of stress on you." I lean his way and my lips brush his forehead. "I love you."

Due to his condition, you postponed the decision to come out to your father, and that's okay. I also know that waiting for the evasive right moment has eaten you alive.

His dad's forced relocation added distance to an already strained relationship. His dad's dreary pursuit of a slightly less challenging career to enable him to go back to work depressed him. His dad's ominous insistence that we not visit until he was fully recovered wounded his son.

"Mike, chill! I'm on your side, here." My hand covers his, sending warmth. Comfort. Tenderness. It's insane how much this man has come to mean to me in so little time. Well, it's been over a year since I finally said the words. Since he finally uttered the words. Since our words finally reflected our actions.

He lets out a pained sigh and glares at the dark green door across the street. A door that will hopefully open up a new opportunity between father and son. "I'm sorry. I figured we'd go in together as a couple because that's what we are."

"Listen, you remember how you didn't want to flaunt your sexual orientation to your friends?" I cock my head to the side. He nods, his eyes losing their focus as he thinks back to Matteo's Halloween party. His edible mouth curls upward dreamily. "It's no different. Since are we interested in making a statement?"

"Mmm… Since never."

"My point exactly. That's not who we are, and that's not about to change. Your father knows you have someone that matters in your life."

"It's more than that, Troy. I *love* you. He needs to know that."

"You're right. But considering who he is, I suggest that we don't enter holding hands like we initially planned. You know as well as I do that he has no clue that you're bringing a dude to Thanksgiving dinner."

"Well, tough luck! He'd better get used to it. Otherwise—"

I clear my throat to cut him off and appease his racing mind. "The idea isn't to deny who or what we are. You're his son. I'm suggesting that you reach out to him first. Give him a chance to adjust to a situation that he's not prepared for. Be the responsible one, even though he wasn't there for you when he should have been. Talk to him, get to know his new wife a little better."

"Sure, I could do that." He rolls up his sleeve to check this watch. My heart melts at the mundane gesture; who has a watch in this day and age when a smart phone does everything for you? "Traffic was so light, we're a half hour early."

"Perfect! I've always wanted to check out the famous Cheers pub on Beacon Street anyway." The air lightens; it's about time! I force a laugh. It's for the best, but I feel like a traitor for recommending that Mike approach his father solo. I fidget in the passenger seat. "I'll have a beer and you just text me whenever. If it goes well, I'll meet you back here."

"If not, we'll go home and I'll do you." The bastard doesn't even blink while I shoot him a salacious look. The air grows suffocating, filled with sexual tension. He knocks the wind out of me, baffled by the nonchalance with which he alluded that he's ready to top. "Either way, as much as I enjoy bottoming, I swear to God, as soon as we get home, I want to save a horse and ride my favorite cowboy... cowboy style. With your fucking cowboy hat on... If that's okay with you, that is."

Our sex life is anything but tame. Yet, this is the one thing that Mike's been hesitant to try, claiming that he didn't want to risk hurting me. Maybe nicknaming him Big Dick Richie was a mistake after all!

At the thought, a knot of pleasure coils tighter and tighter. My lungs seize, and I gawk while trying to gather my wits, to no avail.

He takes that as his cue to nibble on my lips. Whimpering, the sparks fly between us. Heat flares and goosebumps spread across my skin.

Desperately needing to be closer, I moan and scoot towards the driver seat where his firm and enticing body awaits. I rub my cheek against his; it's rare for both of us to be clean-shaven, but the occasion called for extreme measures. My hand caresses his side over the fabric of his preppy oatmeal-colored sweater.

Being parked on this residential street prevents us from making out in the car. Nevertheless, his teasing tongue sweeps into my hungry mouth. We dance. We explore. We play. He tastes like happiness. Desire. Love. Our kiss is heady, and our nerves calm by the time that we come up for air. Enthralled, I didn't realize that his hand traveled to my hair.

My hard-on begs for release, and as far as I can see, so does the bulge in his navy dress pants. Frustrated for a whole other reason now, we shrug and chuckle.

Pupils dilated, we catch our breath, and I slide back to the passenger seat.

"Look, Mike…" I start after a moment. The air shifts again, and I regret that I'm responsible for it. "I'm saying this because I fucked up years ago and let my parents decide how I fit into their family. I was young, stubborn, and proud. I'd hoped that they'd come around; they didn't. I haven't talked to them in over a decade." At last, my confession tumbles from my mouth. My eyes capture his. Lust has been replaced with confusion. "They caught me making out with someone they considered to be the wrong person for their prodigal son. I was shunned and sent to live with my aunt. You see, I have younger siblings who I'm dead to." His face falls.

Way to kill the mood, Hunter!

I carry on. "I didn't mention it because the topic still pisses me off, even after all this time." My beautiful man's cheeks redden and he opens his mouth to speak, but there's no sound. "It's too late. Don't get me wrong, I've learned to live with it." I shrug at the bitterness in my voice. No matter how many years pass, the scars of my youth resurface on occasion. "I was hoping you could benefit from my experience and not make the same mistakes. A door should be opened or closed." I will myself to curb my emotions and bite my lip so forcefully that it draws blood. "It's not easy." I swallow the lump that's now lodged in my throat. "The in-between is what kills people softly." Mike's brows furrow. I'm not a mind-reader, and yet, I follow his train of thought. "I've already told you, being bi never meant we... *I* failed at choosing. It's the complete opposite. I *chose* to be myself. I *chose* to live without compromise. I *chose* to let go of my fears and be with the person I love. And I love you." Once again, I kiss his mouth, then whisper, "I know you have an awesome relationship with your mom, but he's your father. Give him a choice to accept who you are. You two deserve a chance to settle your differences and move on. One way or another."

Before I know it, his powerful hand cups the back of my head and softly draws my forehead to his. His thumb strokes my cheek, sending a whirlwind of lustful sensations that have no place in this moment. His muttered words warm my soul. "Thank you. I'll be back... soon."

After a short stroll, I'm nursing my Sam Adams at the bar while my lover unloads his excess baggage.

I'm on my second beer when the door opens, letting the icy November air filter inside, making me wish I hadn't taken my coat off and laid it across my lap.

"Nice to meet you, Troy Hunter." A commanding voice I

don't recognize intrigues me, and I turn my head to face an older version of the man that I love; and here I thought that Mike's handsome face came by way of his mother, when he took the best of both worlds. Only Mike's beauty is unique due to its raw appeal and blatant sensuality.

His extended hand is a peace offering I hadn't anticipated. He's not smiling, but his face isn't aloof either, which I interpret as a good sign, considering Mike's relaxed stance. Rubbing the back of my neck, I stare at the men with my heart in my throat. I take a deep breath and slide off of the barstool to properly greet the man. "Likewise, Mr. Clayton."

We shake hands.

"Please, call me Edward." I nod at his suggestion. "Do you mind if we join you so you don't have to rush to finish your beer?" We proceed and make small talk. Mike manages to fill in the blanks. Saying that the conversation flows would be far-fetched, but I can tell that Mike's father is doing his best, which he confirms shortly after. "I'm... I'm sorry, it'll take some getting used to." He insists on paying the bill. I thank him and tell him that I understand.

We walk back to his Beacon Hill brownstone in comfortable silence. Mike and I linger a few steps behind as his father opens the door. In a whisper, my lover says, "It went okay. He's okay. We're okay," then pecks my cheek. "Thanks for your advice. I have one complaint, though." I stiffen, although his arm snaking around my waist usually has the opposite effect. "Your favorite little game of this or that was biased. Wrong. Flawed. There was never a choice..." He shakes his head, his eyes full of mischief. "Or rather, the choice is obvious!"

Despite the upcoming snarky comment I sense, I play along. "Oh, really? And what is that?"

"You."

BONUS EPILOGUE – ONE MAN GUY

Mike

SIX MONTHS LATER

S hifting his balance from one foot to the other—to keep moving in New York's brutal January weather— Troy's face contorts, feigning outrage. "I can't believe you gave me a hickey this morning!" He closes the bar door behind him, locks it, and remains on the threshold, as if intimidated. At once, we're immersed in complete silence, a stark contrast to Manhattan's crowded 8th Street, although it's the middle of the afternoon on a weekday.

I shoot him a sideways glance and plaster on my signature poker face. "Did my wicked ways numb you so much that your skillful mouth's been forced shut this whole time?" My voice echoes in the empty space; I can't wait until the new barstools and furniture arrive tomorrow.

"Ha-ha! How old are you, twelve?" I don't miss his sarcasm as we deposit our backpacks on the waxed concrete floor. He takes off his beanie and softly—but uselessly since we're wearing several layers of clothes—punches my bicep. "Claire kept shooting me a knowing look while we played *Monster Hunter* before lunch. I became suspicious, but it took me a trip to the bathroom to figure it out. Thanks for that, moron!"

I muster my most serious tone as my fingers fumble with the zipper of my winter coat and stow my own beanie in my pocket. "Who would have thought that they'd name a video game after my famous boyfriend?"

Paired with a grin, his irritated grumbling is cute. "You know my stage name has nothing to do with it. I didn't know the game existed at the time." He shakes his head. "For the record, you suck at redirecting the conversation. Your diversion sucks. And—"

"If you're about to say that I suck at sucking you off, that's it! You won't benefit from my recently acquired talents any longer." Shrugging, I pout. "Too bad... Just when I nailed my gag reflex."

"Is that blackmail, Clayton?"

"Oh, I wouldn't dare, baby! You know how much I enjoy it when you fuck my mouth." My words make him blush; bingo! Lost in his thoughts, he stares at the exposed beams of the industrial-style ceiling. "You look hot with my hickey, baby." This grants me a gentle smile. I melt and lick my lips suggestively. "What can I say? Branding you felt right today."

My lover swats my ass over my heavy jacket to get me moving. I smirk at him and lead the way towards the large square counter, which sits in the middle of the also square-shaped bar. "Anyway, it's still fun to feel like I'm twelve sometimes, especially when I'm messing with you."

Hand in hand, we walk around like we own the place. Content. Proud. Happy. In sync, we let out a sigh and take everything in. Oooh, wait! We *do* own the place! *This* is ours. *That* makes me giddy.

Soon, Troy stuns me by changing course. "Listen, I'm sorry I never thanked you for choosing me over your fashion career."

"What are you talking about?" My hip slams Troy into a corner by a vintage jukebox.

My jukebox. Music's played such an important role in our lives; when I saw this little gem at an auction, I bought it on a whim, days prior to officially owning this place. Like my mom would say, it was a good omen. I'm immensely pleased with the object and the music selection. It contrasts with the modern ambiance and adds the perfect cozy twist. We plan to set up a makeshift dance floor nearby... soon.

"Troy, you were the one who dropped your rock star status and quit traveling the world to stay close to my ravenous body." I chuckle, then pepper kisses on the hollow of his appetizing neck. His coat slides from his shoulders as he writhes under my ministrations. It remains suspended halfway between his body and the floor as his hands move up to caress my side. I let out a frustrated groan and drop my own parka in one fell swoop.

Our bar. Now that the never-ending paperwork is filled out. Now that our shark of a liquor license lawyer fought tooth and nail for us to be able to sell craft beer alongside more traditional fare. Now that our beloved—and stressful—community board understood that the new venue would be an asset to the area, close enough to Studio 45 to go there more often than not. Our bar, at last. Not a sports bar filled with testosterone, like the one on the cruise. Not a Happy Days-themed bar either, since we couldn't play the part. Just a friendly local bar with quality alcohol and—hopefully—cool people to match.

"Oh, come on, my DJing gave me *some* opportunities." His breathing hitches when my hands land on his shoulder blades and begin their descent towards his sumptuous ass; his useless coat lands at his feet. "That much is true, Mike, but you know as well as I do that I wasn't special enough to make it last."

His dreams. With Troy constantly being on the road, who would have guessed that his dreams were made of brick and mortar? First, his Park Slope bachelor pad and now this. Apparently, none of it represents a sacrifice to him because it feels right. *We* feel right. Before we discussed it, he'd planned to use up all of his music savings. No way Jose! Starting this entrepreneurial adventure on equal footing grounded us. As soon as I stepped in to offer him a second opinion, I fell in love with the atmosphere of the place.

This calls for a celebration! Neither of us drank a drop of the bottle of Dom Pérignon that we brought with us, and yet, we're high on excitement, relief, and hope that it'll grow into a successful business.

"Untrue," I retort. "You are *very* special to me. Plus, *we* make it last, whether I'm on my knees or not." I emphasize the words and snicker at my own comeback.

"Ain't you a sweet talker?"

"That's how I got Monster Hunter hooked, wasn't it?" I wink.

"Right… Your inebriated hitting on Anna was sooo sexy!" I open my mouth to counter to no avail. "Anyway, I appreciate the praise, but one record deal isn't enough to float this six-figure joint." A furrow forms between his eyebrows. No matter how relieved he is that everything worked according to plan, I can tell that he's only half-joking.

"Oh, please… I beg to differ, baby. Musically, Matteo and tons of others think you are the bomb. Is that why my lucky bastard of a best friend will get to attend some of your private sessions whenever you decide to give it a go again?" He nods and grants me easier access to his jawline for more TLC. "Maybe you should have given it more time." My statement sounds like a question.

"Again, it's endearing that, after all this time, you're still sugarcoating my future in music you don't know the first thing about. I love you." I nibble on his earlobe as my way to call bullshit.

Troy Hunter isn't a phase. My uptight father managed to deal with the fact that love is love, but I've heard hurtful and heinous words and shaming when some realize that Troy and I are a couple. Why people feel entitled to share their opinions on the sexual preferences of others is beyond me. Troy and I are in this together. In turn, I made the easy decision to adjust my career path that I wrongly believed was my dream. It took a few twists and turns to find my true calling, which is less glamorous than Fashion Week, but it suits me. Troy embodies everything I'd unconsciously wanted without admitting it to myself: someone to love unconditionally and who loves me back just as much... and a job opportunity to go along with it. Thanks to my man's management skills, I'm excited about the challenge that awaits us, especially knowing that his former boss at his most recent bartending gig showed him the ropes.

"Still, you haven't lost your touch…"

He interrupts me as I knew he would. "And yes, you make me…" He pauses for a split second, then unabashedly snatches one of my hands to place it on his throbbing erection. Of course, he had to make it sexual! "Hard." Worrying his bottom lip with his front teeth, he wraps his hand around mine and squeezes. "And no, I definitely haven't lost my touch." With a low voice that's infused with lust, my boyfriend pins me with a matching stare. My pulse accelerates as I read the unspoken promises in it. "Thanks for that, Mike." He smirks playfully. I love this side of him… What am I saying? I love every side of him! "Right back at you, filthy beast!"

"Says the guy who calls me Big Dick Richie…" I trail off.

"Only when your dick wants in my ass, and you know you won't hear any complaints on my part!" He wiggles his eyebrows.

"Ha-ha." My face reddens as I remember my first time inside him. Exactly as planned: Him, with his cowboy hat on. Me, cowboy style. We needed to blow off some steam after Thanksgiving. I was so fucking scared to hurt him, though. Thankfully, after lots of prep work, it was such a rewarding experience. Since then, our sex and day-to-day life continue to be more fulfilling. We know that we don't have to fix each other. We're so compatible, it's otherworldly. We make so much sense together, it's ridiculous. We're so in love, it's insane... Porn takes place between our sheets now, not on a screen—or much less so—and I welcome his initiative as he welcomes my curiosity. Lately, he upped our game with a couple of toys that my imagination hadn't fathomed!

Out of the blue, his tone turns serious. "Let's make a deal. You'll ignore my this or that, and I'll stop referring to your monster dick and mentioning your resemblance to Channing Tatum. I'll pretend that I never noticed either as long as I can enjoy the man I love and his... attributes?" I groan my agreement, and his playfulness returns. "Who would have thought it'd be so easy to jump-start your sex drive?"

"What can I say? I was hooked the second you shoved your tongue down my throat." We chuckle, and his breath seizes as my hand moves more quickly along his crotch.

With that shamelessly stolen kiss in Paris, he put me under his spell. It's as if he pours everything he has into his spellbinding kisses that I can't get enough of.

The mind reader's hungry mouth assaults mine in the best of ways, claiming an urgent kiss that I gladly welcome. His lips mold with mine like two pieces of a not-so-complex puzzle, and my arm snakes around his waist to yank him closer. The delicious friction of our jean-clad cocks heats the skin behind my neck. I quiver in bliss. My lover fists my wavy hair, making my scalp prickle under his fiery touch.

"Mmm..." Yeah, I've attended the most elite boarding schools that the world has to offer, and that's how eloquent the fucker renders me!

Leonard Cohen's *I'm Your Man* fills the place while I get reacquainted with the taste of his commanding lips. I'm a starved man when it comes to his affection. His five-o'clock shadow grazes against mine which sends shivers down my spine. The fast tempo of my romantic heart and my aching manhood can attest that my craving for this man isn't about to be tamed.

Regretfully, I break the salacious kiss to come up for air. "*You* make me horny, Troy Hunter. Every. Fucking. Minute." So, maybe not so romantic after all.

"You know what? I want to do something special."

"Oh, yeah? What's that?"

"You." My index finger points at his chiseled chest. "I wanna do *you*, Troy Hunter." My gaze stays focused on his. My breathing doesn't falter. My body shows undeniable approval. I'm confident in my own skin; my first encounter with him was only the first step of many that I yearn to take with the man that I fell head over heels for.

"Here? Now, you mean?"

"Nah, I'm not that... brave, but as soon as we're done here." I close my eyes, and when they pop open, I sputter, suddenly hesitant for no valid reason; this guy knows me inside and out.

"Well, I think we're done then. Let's go!"

"Wait!" I take a deep breath to gather my wits. "Forever. I want to be..."

His brown eyes are expectant. "You want to be what, Mike Clayton?"

My body hums at the way we eye-fuck each other. "What I always was." I never want it to stop. I swallow my last bit of hesitation because he needs to know how much he means to me.

"Yours."

THE END

Dear Reader,

I hope you enjoyed **This or That: An Enemies-To-Lovers MM Romance**. Hearing from you is very important to me and I value your opinion, so feel free to connect with me on my website, social media. Please consider leaving your feedback on **Goodreads** or wherever you purchased this book. Reviews are a great way to let other readers know what to read next and are precious for indie authors. Thanks for reading!
Hope.

This or That is a standalone prequel to *Omega Artist* (A Cocky Hero Club Novel).
For a glimpse at Mike and Troy's future together and to visit some familiar faces, start *Omega Artist* today.

And if you want to know more about the magic surrounding the mysterious murders in Boston and the ancient Irish legend spurring them, then *The Perry Witches' Legacy series* is for you… Michael Clayton is wrong; it's not bullshit or folklore at all.
(Note that the series was formerly published as The Black Angel Book Legend series.)

Also, if you haven't met Brandon Boner yet, you should definitely check him out and read *Changing His Game* by Justine Elvira. I enjoyed this unique character so much that I asked for permission to borrow him. Permission granted, and I'm so proud!

To keep up with all the latest, follow Hope on social media or *join **Hope's mailing list** for a FREE book as a welcome gift, exclusive book information and great deals.*

KEEP READING for a sneak peek at ***Omega Artist*** (A Cocky Hero Club novel) **and *The Perry Witches' Legacy series, #1: Cursed Calligrapher*. Find out more now!**

OMEGA ARTIST (A COCKY HERO CLUB NOVEL)

SNEAK PEEK

PROLOGUE - NO WOMAN NO CRY

TIG

"You're gonna be late." My brow knits. "Again." I can't resist smacking Delia's plump ass playfully. Bewildered, she shrieks and jumps, giggling, and her long dark curls follow.

Bob is singing per usual, filling our Brooklyn apartment with perfect vibes. It's been settled for years: the day that Delia graces me with a child, whether it's a he or a she, the kid's name will be Marley. Plain and simple. No second thoughts.

"I'm never late!" My wife flips me the bird, her big brown eyes dancing with glee. Damn, I adore this fiery woman! We're not even thirty, and over twelve years have already passed since our first kiss. Right in the middle of our small colorful kitchen, I lean her way and plant a kiss on her cheek. She immediately relaxes. "I make a point to be early when it's a new venue."

Agitated, she swipes her oversized purse from the kitchen

stool and scurries out of the room to find her car keys, and when I hear the telltale sound of a zipper, a smile tugs at my lips.

I'm familiar with all of her little idiosyncrasies by now. I cherish all of her little habits by now. I revel in all of her little obsessions by now. Buying mostly organic is one. Daring me to do something insanely stupid every Friday the thirteenth another. Misplacing her car keys is also typical.

Meanwhile, I've been cleaning up after our Saturday breakfast: dishes in the dishwasher, food in the cabinets, juice in the fridge… And, of course, the coffee pot is still hot.

Delia's deep voice tears me out of my reverie. I shake my head to escape my trip down memory lane; I often get stuck inside my head, and our late night doesn't help me focus on the present. Smiling, I look in her direction only to register that her light jacket is already on and she's ready to depart. I take a deep breath, and the mixed aromas of coffee, weed, and her unique feminine fragrance suddenly assault my nostrils.

Yesterday's party definitely took its toll on our beauty sleep; Delia and I don't smoke like we used to, but we enjoy a rare joint on special occasions. Needless to say, Soraya and especially Mr. Big Prick—I mean Soraya's husband Graham—disapprove, but yesterday evening fit the bill.

"The distance to middle of nowhere upstate New York won't be an issue, trust me. And if you'd talk less, I could actually go pick up Soraya."

"Oh, right! I forgot that she was tagging along."

"Well, she basically begged me, claiming that she needed a break from Lorenzo." I seem to remember her telling me that they'll get back home late tomorrow afternoon. "He's barely a year old!" Delia's famous for exaggerating: Lorenzo's eighteen months old. "Who'd want to abandon that adorable boy's side for more than a second?"

"Our best friend, apparently." My wit earns me a sloppy kiss in haste, and I slap her ass again as it disappears behind the door.

Her last words resonate through the door. "Shame on her!"

The tornado that is my lovely wife is away for the weekend, piercing strangers' body parts that I'm not eager to tally, and shortly after, I'm off to Tig's Tattoo and Piercing. Yeah, yeah, we should've come up with something more original or witty to name the tattoo parlor that we co-own on Eighth Avenue!

Well, we couldn't agree for once, so on a drunken night prior to our opening years ago, Soraya suggested putting names on scraps of paper and picking one at random. Work ethic, a safe environment, and word-of-mouth have helped our small family-owned business to thrive. We've considered renaming it, but success picked up quickly, and it'd be counterproductive at this point. Given Delia's efforts to boost our online presence, the name will definitely stick.

The drizzle that covers my face when I exit the subway annoys me. Thankfully, it's only a short walk.

"Thanks for opening the parlor for me, Claire," I say in a cheerful voice, waving to the tall girl with long purple dread-locks. "Sorry for running late this morning. Delia's little adventure didn't help. She always takes forever to get ready and worries that she'll forget something. And you know the drive makes her nervous, especially with this unpredictable November weather. I'm just hoping that Soraya will be behind the wheel." My wife is such a crazy driver—typical Jersey girl!

Laughing at the thought, I peel off my wet coat and am about to head to the back of the shop when Claire nods and replies, "No problem." She's never been talkative, but she's damn good at her job.

I check my watch and grumble to myself, "Where the fuck are you, Marco?" I hate when my cousin's late. He obviously cares since he was the one to offer to hold down the fort until we find a hostess. We had a temp who stole from us when we first filled the position, and we've had a hard time trusting the appli-cants since. Luckily, Marco was out of a job at the time and stepped in… I probably shouldn't be glad about his jobless situation, but I am! Not that I'll ever admit that to him, though.

I take a look around, paying special attention to make sure that nothing's missing from the stations where Claire and I will be working today. Out of habit, I take my rings off to wash my hands.

We take pride in giving each client the best experience possible. You see, Delia and I usually work hand in hand, so to speak; she handles the piercings and I work on tats. She lives for these gigs—fairs, conventions, and markets—and this one gives her and Soraya a chance for some solo girl time, which has been more sporadic lately. My wife and I are happy to share our best friend, and Soraya is adamant that she instantly gained a friend when I grew closer to Delia in junior high.

Back then, I was relieved that the two of them hit it off, and now we're glad that sassy Soraya has found her significant other. Prior to Graham, her romantic life was a challenge which she blamed on being a loser magnet rather than on her Italian smart mouth. Yes, our best friend has her hands full with her busy high-maintenance husband, their baby son, and Graham's daughter, Chloe, who spends her weekends with them so that she can stay with her mom on weekdays for school.

My own life was the polar opposite; from the moment that I set eyes on the curvy Delia, I knew that I would belong to her forever. I'd be lost without her in my life. There isn't a day that we don't bicker like teenagers, because we love it. There isn't a day that we don't want to be together, because we love it. There isn't a day that we don't enjoy working side-by-side, because we love it.

Our booming business recently required two adjustments to accommodate more clients. The first one is to our schedule, adding Sunday morning walk-in appointments, which allows us to hire some regular help, like Claire, here and there. The second one is the pro bono customers—that Delia refers to as survivors

—that I gladly help, whether they're victims of violence or self-harm or recovering patients.

I walk back up front and nod at Marco, who finally retrieved his pretty face from his muscular ass and made it here. I pretend to scold him as Claire leads her first client of the day to her work area.

Moments later, the bell over the door rings and a quiet dark-haired girl in her early twenties comes in, eyes glued to her feet and swirling her perfectly groomed straight hair around her index finger. Next thing I know, her Burberry rain jacket lands on the coat rack. A couple more steps, and she pauses to assess the place before settling on us. Then, her eyes return to her riding boots in record time; they'd be more at home on Fifth Avenue, but what do I know about all that?

I don't miss the raunchy once-over that she gives me, nor do I miss the flush that colors her pale face. Marco elbows me, and I regret that he saw that too.

Trust me, I'm flattered by the attention I get. All the same, her game is clear: everything about her screams preppy girl in search of an adventure.

"Hello, my name's Sybil…" I have the hardest time understanding her last name, but I don't interrupt. "I have an appointment today." Her accent is strong. Her nervous smile is painful. Her obvious cluelessness is endearing.

Marco and I exchange a knowing glance; despite making the first move, her face wears a wild expression that proves her bravery has limits. That's why the fact that she already made an appointment puzzles me. Usually, the first step is either to chat with us via our website or social media, call, or pay us a visit.

Interesting…

"I have an appointment," she repeats, "with…" She stares alternatively between me and Marco. In spite of the family resemblance, if she checked our website, she shouldn't be mistaken. She retrieves the latest iPhone from her Prada purse—

is she the devil in disguise or what?—"Tig," she announces, reading the information from said phone.

"You must be my 10:30. Welcome, I'm Tig."

She extends her hand for me to shake, which I'm not used to, and the second our eyes actually meet, she averts my gaze to her feet again and her face turns beet red.

Embarrassment. Shyness. Infatuation… At least, that's what Delia claims, and she's probably right. My creative wife has her own take on this common occurrence that I still struggle with. Having clients check us out is apparently part of the job. Admiring the works of art that are our bodies is apparently part of the job. Being interested in our appearances is apparently part of the job. Anyway, I'm not bragging, but clients do check me out. A lot.

To be honest, most people would prefer picture-perfect Graham, with his expensive suits and CEO look, over me.

Don't get me wrong, I'm well aware that I have the reckless bad boy vibe going on. The tats. The height. The attitude. And let's not forget that I'm an artist. That's where the true appeal lies, I think. Add to this that I'm far from repulsive… minus one tiny detail (and I'm not talking about my dick!).

"Do you have anything in mind?"

"Yes… no… I'm a virgin, you know." It's my turn to blush at her blunt revelation. Suddenly, we're in a cartoon. She's Little Red Riding Hood and we're the wolves. What the hell was that?

"Fuck me!" My cousin's jaw drops so low it almost hits the counter. It's not an invitation, though she's attractive, rather an expression of his utter shock.

"Shut up, Marco." I slap his bulging bicep. He deserves it. Why else would he wear a short-sleeve tee-shirt the weekend before Thanksgiving, except to show off his ridiculously impressive muscles?

At once, her hands go flying in denial. "No, no, no, I didn't mean it like that." Somehow, I'm relieved, although I shouldn't really care. She's addressing me, holding my gaze this time. "I meant to say that I'm a virgin… tattoo-wise. I don't have a single one." She shrugs. "I'm here to rectify that."

"Can I see some ID?"

"Wow, you're a buzzkill, Mister Tig!"

"Mister Tig?" Marco exclaims. "If anyone in the family could portray Mister T, it would be me!" She offers him a small smile. "Hey, I'm Marco." He clearly finds her to his liking. But he's aware of the rule: no messing with the customers until their follow-up appointment.

To cut this conversation short—mostly the part that involves Marco—after checking her French passport, I grab a couple of folders filled with samples of my work that might give her some ideas and stroll towards the back.

"Follow me." I hear her footsteps keep pace without another word. Once she's sitting across from me, she browses through the designs and starts babbling between my explanation of the process and our exchange regarding her choice of design and location. She's here for a family funeral. She's part American on her mother's side. She's a Parisian who intends to study in the U.S.

"I'm sorry, I guess talking helps calm my nerves."

"No problem." I listen to her for a bit more, and we discuss her options. After showing her a few pictures, she settles on a small bird escaping from a cage, to be placed on the right side of her inner thigh.

O-kay.

First, I sketch it so that we agree on the style and proportions.

"Let's do this." Her voice sounds shaky. Her tone rings too excited. Her words seem forced. But as soon as they leave her mouth, her body relaxes, so I snap on my gloves and get down to business.

I can't wait to see Delia tomorrow for our dinner date!

The entire time, she pours out her life story that I listen to absentmindedly, but I mostly concentrate on work.

I miss Delia like crazy right now!

Her oppressive father hates tattoos. This will be her dirty little secret...

Dirty is my plan after our dinner date!

This isn't the first time that a client's mistaken me for a shrink. I don't mind the confession, but it's not my job, so I nod, shrug, and mumble.

Damn, my life is so simple compared to yours, miss!

Once I'm done, she tugs on her designer jeans, hugs me and mutters a thank you into my ear, and flees the confined space. Her intimate gesture unsettles me.

"I'm a sucker for heavily tattooed men," she whispers.

It's not much of a leap, considering that several swirls escape from my collar, and who would do that if not tattooed elsewhere, right?

Refusing to acknowledge her flirting, I peel my gloves off and go wash my hands in the corner of the small room, where I'm startled to find my rings sitting beside the sink. I must have been extremely preoccupied to forget to put them back on. I do now.

And that's when she sees it, the tiny detail: my wedding band. Instantly, her eyes widen, and she bites her lip, but she doesn't comment. Why would she?

Prior to dashing out of the parlor to join Marco, who's outside smoking, she says, "I'm glad that I chose you to take my virginity," between clenched teeth.

Sure, whatever.

See what I said about the bad boy appeal? And I would never take advantage of it because I'm married and adore my wife. Because I voiced my vows and have no intention of breaking them. Because I'll always belong to one woman, until death do us part.

While Delia's gone, I don't hear much from her, aside from a few texts. Either way, we're not one of those couples who spends hours glued to our phones when we're apart.

As much as I'm looking forward to hearing about the fun she's having, I bet she's swamped with work and I refrain from calling her both Saturday and Sunday.

Remember, she said something about the crappy connection anyhow.

It won't make much of a difference anyway. Her side of the bed will only be cold for one night, so I sprawl in the middle to keep it warm. Must be why I'm dragging when I wake up on Sunday. Thank God, work is great and flies by, but I still miss her and am eager to catch up at tonight's reunion.

Yes, can't wait for our date!

When I'm done with work, I grab lunch and spend the entire afternoon working on a new painting.

It's pretty nice, yet a part of my stupid heart feels empty without her near me.

I had been on a painting hiatus for months, which somehow dissolved when I came back from the parlor today. My tension has vanished. My heart has grown lighter. My mood has settled on joyful.

I scrub off the paint stains, get changed in no time, and hurry to our usual neighborhood spot.

Unfortunately, I'm facing an empty chair.

According to the oversized clock at the Heights Cafe, she's already forty minutes late. I curse quietly and fidget in my seat while pouring another glass of their featured wine of the month to relax.

My first two texts were mainly to check on my two favorite girls; I intentionally don't call when she's driving.

I worry the corner of my lip with my canine tooth, shooting her a third one as I grow more worried by the second. This isn't like her, and a bad connection can't be an excuse any longer. I scratch the back of my head and shake it at Hugh, the waiter, as he approaches to take my order.

One sip of wine later, my thoughts clear, and an idea strikes me.

"Hey, Soraya."

"Tig, 'sup?" I hear a baby crying in the background. She asks me to hold on, yells at Graham to take the baby, and gets back on the line. "So sorry that I couldn't make it this weekend, I wish I could've gone to Woodstock with Del."

Wait, what?

Why is she home? Why is she talking to Graham? Why isn't she with Delia? My agitation skyrockets, and I rush out of the restaurant to have this conversation while pacing on the street, thankful that the rain has stopped.

"What do you mean, you couldn't make it? Delia never mentioned that you bailed on her." I'm freezing since I stupidly left my coat inside, but my sudden numbness is a perfect shield against the cold weather. On top of that, my heart is beating so fucking fast that my lungs seize.

"I'm sorry, Tig. Lorenzo's sick, so I couldn't go. Del called and got someone from the convention to sub for me." My friend pauses, and I hear a distinct swallow on the other end of the line. "She isn't back yet?" Her voice mirrors my concern. "But she should have been back at least an hour ago!"

"I know." My strangled voice can't do much more than tell her that I have to go and will keep her posted.

I call her. Voicemail. I text her. No reply. I implore her. No use. I leave the restaurant, apologizing on my way out, and sprint back home. What the actual fuck? Why isn't she responding to my calls or texts?

That's when I notice it.

One tiny detail on my phone that I didn't pay attention to previously. One alert for a missed call that holds the answer to my future. One missed call that proves that nothing lasts forever. One missed call that changes my life for the worse.

Out of breath, I rush to the hospital to see my wife, only to have the surgeon inform me of my new status.

A widower.

Buy it now - Read for free on KU

Add to your TBR

THE PERRY WITCHES' LEGACY, #1: CURSED CALLIGRAPHER

SNEAK PEEK

CHAPTER 1 - HURT

ROSE

"I don't think that I want you to be the mother of my children."

Wait, what?

Children? Mother? Since when?

"I don't think that I want us to keep seeing each other."

Wait, what?

He thought? He didn't want? Since when?

"I don't think that I want to continue wasting my time with you."

Wait, what?

Wasting his time? With me? Since when? No warning signs. No logical explanations. Nothing.

How lame of him to pull this stunt in such a snide way. I doubted he was in any way interested in what I had to say on the subject. I had just turned twenty-one and there was no purpose in fast-forwarding our relationship. We were fine until a second ago. Why the sudden need to change things between us?

Once these three sentences were blurted out in a matter-of-fact tone, Guillaume parked in front of my mom's Parisian apartment building, near Bastille, and sat quietly to let them sink in. Meanwhile, from the corner of my eye, I noticed that his knuckles were getting whiter and whiter from his tight grip on the wheel. He didn't budge, his deep blue eyes wandering anywhere inside his car but at me.

I readied myself to open the passenger door to escape and hopefully get a good night's sleep. Instead, I froze and stared ahead. No matter how hard I tried to will myself to move, I simply couldn't force myself to look at the man seated in the driver seat.

A chill began to course through my body, and I swallowed down an irrepressible need to throw up. I waited while listening to some depressing English pop song that barely registered as a muffled sound. I heard only *him*.

My thoughts started to ramble at full speed. My way of avoiding the situation and confronting him. He, who sat like a crash test dummy, gripping the fucking wheel even harder as I clutched my purse with the same strength.

I could tell by his sudden cowardice that he would never take any of the words back. Not that he had any intention of doing so. Clearly, he wasn't interested in how his words sounded, or how they would be received, but rather whether they'd hit their target.

Bull's eye.

I had no way of turning back time to undo the pain that was beginning to tighten around my aching heart.

We had a future together, or so I thought. A future that may or may not include children in it, and I had leaned toward *may* rather than *may not*.

Still, it was too soon to be discussed, in my humble opinion.

We were too young. We hadn't been dating long enough. We didn't have steady jobs...

So many reasons for his outburst to leave me speechless.

And most of all, we had never broached the subject, so where did this come from? Since when had children become an issue between us? I couldn't make myself ask, nor did I want any information about a new love interest that he might have found.

Have you been cheating on me, or are you contemplating the thought?

That poisonous thought hit me out of nowhere and stole my breath for a split second. Enough time to make me uncomfortable. Enough time to make me wonder. Enough time to make me nauseous.

The song that was playing rubbed salt into the wound. *Girl Afraid*. And just like the girl in the song, I wondered where did his intentions lay? Only, it was a totally different situation because I was supposed to *know* the boy that was sitting to my left.

I hadn't seen it coming because everything had always been so easy with him. A mutual friend introduced us at a party; back then I was enrolled in my second and final year of a math prep school generally required to enter France's elite schools. He was a first-year student in a prestigious architecture school, ESA.

Although we hit it off right from the start, we took it slow. I chose to put aside my attraction to this good-looking guy with golden blond hair and a strange sense of humor.

Shortly after we realized that the attraction was mutual, we nonetheless decided that it was best to remain friends. I was too driven by my studies and exams, having no spare time to date since my school required loads of work, and after the mandatory two years, I was left exhausted and drained. It had been too demanding, and I felt lost and unable to see my future. I needed a break before prep school ended, so I traveled to Bali.

That was where Guillaume and I hooked up on spring break.

Shortly after we came back to France, he earned his bachelor's degree from ESA. I followed his lead and joined the same school.

Despite what I had told Guillaume, my dream of becoming an architect hadn't been dictated by him, but rather by my late dad, Sean, who had also been an architect.

Shortly after we started dating, I became friends with Guillaume's best friend, Vincente, a tall and slender guy whose mother was from Italy and his father from Vietnam. Despite the closely-shaven hair on either side of his skull, he kept the rest of it long enough to wear in a short ponytail, giving him a unique look that caused everybody to refer to him as Samurai. My favorite Samurai. Outspoken and caring, he was easy to talk to and also the king of lame jokes.

Lame jokes that I had heard over and over again at his party that night. Yet, right this second, none of them came to mind to lighten the mood. And the buzz that I felt from the alcohol swirling through my system didn't do shit to lessen the punch in the guts that Guillaume delivered.

We were on the way back from the party that Vincente threw to celebrate my graduation. A fun party. A bunch of great friends. A happy couple...or not.

His words were pronounced in a loud and clear voice, completely devoid of emotion. I loved his voice. In truth, I was a sucker for deep male voices, and although his didn't quite match these requirements, I loved it nonetheless. Well, at that very moment, I found his voice despicable because of his words.

Such simple phrases. Such poisonous phrases. Such nonsensical phrases.

Slowly but surely, my heart splintered into tiny pieces that were like shrapnel, ready to burst inside of me. Yet I remained silent, at a loss for words that would form an adequate response that could somehow make this okay.

I couldn't wait to go upstairs and cry out the hurt. I prayed that my mom and Chris, my fifteen-year-old brother, would be asleep considering the time. I needed some alone time to process the news that I was incapable of wrapping my head around.

I did a piss-poor job at swallowing the lump that was lodged in my throat, and forced myself not to shed a tear. I wished for the running engine to explode into a wild fireball so that we would die. It didn't.

Emptiness filled me as I continued to listen to him when all I wanted was to open the car door and exit the confined space.

"Trust me, it's better to break up now." His sugary tone worsened his case: what was the use in trying to lessen the impact of how he expressed his callous sentiments? The asshole hadn't looked at me once, too busy searching for the right song to fit his current mood.

The Smiths again, really? Fucking perfect. *Last Night I Dreamt...* Well, so did I, and it didn't involve my boyfriend of two-and-a-half years and first true love dumping me like... like what? I couldn't find it in me to categorize it. Why did Guillaume bring up trust when he had just betrayed the trust that I had placed in him?

Unfortunately, he just wouldn't shut up. "Look, Rose, if we keep this up, we're just going to end up hurting each other."

Don't Rose me, asshole, can't you understand that you've already hurt me?

My entire body shivered violently as if I was taking a freezing cold shower. He continued talking. I continued shuddering uncontrollably. We continued to ignore one another.

"I don't think that I've ever loved you, you know."

The last blow for the kill.

Holy hell.

How could I have imagined falling in love with someone as hard as I had and then falling out of it just as quickly? Actually, that wasn't true. I still loved the conniving bastard with all of my heart and soul. Both parts of myself that, after being smashed, shattered, and broken would never be successfully glued back together. Neither would ever be able to be fixed properly because irreparable damage had been done.

I couldn't take it anymore. I couldn't remain in the same space as him. I couldn't...

Still, he robbed my last thought before I rushed out of the car. As I turned to slam the door shut, I heard him say, "Deal with it..."

Yeah, I couldn't and wouldn't deal with it.

At that, the words of Sean Bateman rang inside my head. I loved Patrick Bateman's brother in *American Psycho* and instantly thought of his favorite expression. "Rock' n' roll," I whispered to myself as my feet hit the sidewalk, and I walked away.

He was gone by the time that I tugged open the building door.

Later, after I let my muted sobs and ugly tears be absorbed by my pillow, the events replayed endlessly before my eyes. Nothing made sense.

Should I be appeased that he was only partially a jerk? At least he didn't use excuses and the easy way out like, "It's not you, it's me. You're a wonderful person, but I'm a mess right now so it's best if we break it off... Let's stay friends, okay?"

For weeks, Guillaume's words haunted me. I couldn't get over the fact that deep inside, I knew that something prompted them but I simply couldn't put my finger on it.

"I don't think that I want you to be the mother of my children."

Words that were said in French but remained engrained in English, my second language. My deceased father's mother tongue. As if playing them over and over in English would lessen the pain.

I was raised in Provincetown, Massachusetts—most people call it P-Town—until I was about four. Then I gathered that my mom judged it to be an unhealthy environment in which to raise a child. So she convinced my dad that Paris was a better option. She said that we should all rejoin her relatives, and she flew her French butt out of there, back where she thought we belonged, with my little butt in tow. Shortly after, my American dad followed us and imposed French as our default language at home… What a weird idea!

I had spent the majority of the past ten summer vacations in P-Town as an attempt to reconnect with my American background in a more carefree environment. There I tried to catch up on my long-lost English language, which had been my mother tongue once upon a time. In fact, I'd have to admit that my slight accent betrayed my French upbringing on some specific words such as three or available.

And as much as I loved France, I hated to constantly be reminded of my accent because, to me, it meant that I no longer belonged in the US despite my American dad. Growing up, I noticed that when I was stressed out, the French language took over. It was considered to be endearing, though I'd say annoying. I could live with that.

Months after Guillaume had broken up with me, his words still hadn't stopped ricocheting inside my head. I gave him my mind, my body and my soul. He mercilessly trampled over each.

"I don't think that I want us to keep seeing each other."

I was a wreck, empty inside. I had to do something to climb from the pit of my bottomless grief. I couldn't bear to be in that state anymore, essentially having the word "depressed" tattooed across my forehead, yet I couldn't help it. A state where I couldn't feel anything. Numb.

A year of loneliness and despair that I had put to good use. My family tried their best to support me, but I was unreachable. My heart was dried as that of a mummy, and nothing could help me to reason my way out of it. That was why I wondered just as much as my mom how I passed my exams without much trouble and earned my bachelor's degree.

"I don't think that I want to continue wasting my time with you."

So that was how I started to cut myself, shortly after Guillaume broke up with me. Soon enough, I discovered that my instincts were correct. Unsurprisingly enough, Guillaume was a cheater. Rumor had it that he had been seeing other people behind my back. Quite a lot of them. Lying son of a bitch!

The bottom line was: men could only be trusted as friends.

Hence, the self-harm. I'd much rather hurt myself than provide someone else the tools to do it, so I used Tiny's forgotten X-Acto knife. My cousin's girlfriend was named Veronica but because of her height and slim body, everybody called her Tiny.

I was grateful that she forgot this precious tool, after having spent a couple of weekends with us in Paris. The twenty-year-old petite woman had been studying numerous techniques in a scriptorium in Toulouse, France: drawing, collage, calligraphy, knotwork and illumination.

I made good use of her blade. Poor desperate little girl.

Out of curiosity, I had questioned my ability to feel something. I did. It hurt. Not too much. The right amount to feel alive, at least. After the first few times the razor blade met the inside of my wrist, I found that I took pleasure in it. I *really* did. I wasn't trying to kill myself, I swear. I hid the marks under a large leather triquetra wristband that Guillaume had given me on our first anniversary.

The irony wasn't lost on me that all I had left of him was his meaningful gift which I used to hide the wounds of our broken love under a Trinity knot, the Celtic triangle that symbolized past, present and future—as if I had a future with him!

The wounds didn't heal fast enough, but nobody ever noticed. Then it became an addiction. I had to do it. To remember how to feel. Some cuts here and there? Well, my body and mind were in pieces so what difference did it make? I was a zombie anyway.

For the first time, I found it impossible to admit to Judd, my favorite American cousin, what I'd been doing to myself. I had been such a fool... Learning to cope with bad experiences and rejection were part of growing up, right? I understood that now.

The one good thing I got from the breakup had been Vincente's undying friendship. We had become inseparable around the time that things went down the drain with Guillaume, and he stood by me, always. And to be sure that my intentions were clear I made a bold move and set Vincente up on a blind date—not a typical French tradition—with Alexandra, another friend of mine. I was proud of my matchmaking talents because they've been together ever since.

Perhaps I wasn't ready to commit because my parents had met at a young age, didn't wait to get married, and had this perfect relationship, setting my expectations too high? Perhaps it was because I wasn't ready yet with Guillaume?

It took forever to figure things out. It took daily self-harming. It took my loss of trust in men. But I did it. Finally, I fathomed that as much as I was hurting, I could still rationalize our break-up. Because, you see, I've always been a rational girl and that was how I coped with pain. I let it engulf me for a moment after which I completely ignored it and pretended that it never existed.

So, in a way, our break-up helped me to not waste additional years with Guillaume. It was safe to say that even after a year, I was still a ghost. Still, the ghost was thankful that he had dumped me: not how he actually handled it, but somehow that he found whatever consciousness he had to articulate the thought and eventually spat it out.

A ghost, and my mother, Isabelle, found a way to get rid of me for a few months and offer me a great vacation at the same time. A smart move. Only I never predicted what an impact her decision would have on my life. I would have called you a liar if you had warned me about what would follow.

The irony of it was that this American vacation was supposed to get rid of the Guillaume syndrome, as my mom had put it, yet Guillaume loathed the US, despite the fact that he had never set foot there. Narrow-minded, he assumed what some uninspired French people believed to be true: the America portrayed on TV was the real deal... as if. So glad it wasn't true since TV never truly captures reality but portrays the extreme for entertainment. Stupid and clueless Guillaume.

P-Town would be a cure for me. Of course, that was the rational part of me speaking after the emotional nerve-wracking part exploded in France a year ago. The hurt was still palpable, and I simply couldn't get over it. I had to admit I was still equally appalled by his betrayal and my gullibility.

It took time to build a strong relationship, but it took him a minute to end it. Breaking up was rarely a smooth ride, but I had taken it the harshest way possible because Guillaume had handled the situation poorly and betrayed me. Still, I couldn't let go and continued to cherish and reminisce about most of our time together, even though I understood that he turned out to be wrong for me. Far away from my French troubles, my helpless mother thought that I would be willing to revel in a long summer vacation the best I could.

Thanks, Mom, for booking a flight to Boston to take me out of my misery.

Deep in her heart, my mom would have trusted Aunt Lana with her own life, it was the same for me and Judd. My rebel of a cousin remained my hero in the US; I was thrilled to see him during the summer.

Before my parents and I went back to live in Paris, I considered him to be my older brother, and people would say that we were joined at the hip. We kind of looked alike as well, sharing the dark wavy hair and greenish-brown eyes that ran in the family. The difference now was his height and build. Where he was a surfer type—not too tall, but muscular—my figure was slimmer; his thick dark hair was cut short while mine was shoulder length with a few highlights peeking through here and there. Other than our resemblance and our love of scary movies —the cheesier, the better—we were nothing alike. He was a hard-working self-made man while I was a depressed struggling student. He was a clown while I was a square. He was bisexual while I was straight.

Every time I came back to P-Town, he was in some sort of trouble for not studying, stealing, smoking pot... Maybe I liked him because he was a rebel. Maybe he was my evil twin, after all. Maybe we completed each other perfectly, and that was why we enjoyed a strong connection.

I was well aware that my aunt and my cousin were the only ones who could reasonably cope with me, considering my state of mind for the past year.

I drifted off to sleep, and hoped that I would be able to thank her for sending me. I was tired of being lost. I was tired of being numb. I was tired of being myself.

Granted, I had interpreted her decision as a punishment at first, but deep down I understood that it wasn't. I had waited too long to go back there. I've always felt good there. I've always felt free there. I've always felt alive there.

That didn't happen anymore.

Guillaume took that away from me, without even compre-hending the damage he'd done. I had placed my trust in him, faith even, but he fucked it all up. Somehow, our failure made me doubt men. I was hopeless now, certain that I wouldn't ever have a meaningful relationship.

Happily ever after?

Not for me, but Vincente and Alexandra found love, so deep down, I had a glimmer of hope. Those two were getting married this winter. But it was only May, and at this point, I wasn't looking forward to attending that wedding. I wasn't looking forward to facing Guillaume again. I wasn't looking forward to showing how affected and alone I still was.

My mind and my body, yearning for the daily rush of the blade, kept reminding me that I was far from cured.

Crushed.

The series is complete & free to read with Kindle Unlimited

Add to your TBR

THIS OR THAT - PLAYLIST ON SPOTIFY

1 – I Walk the Line: Johnny Cash

2 – When Bad Does Good: Chris Cornell

3 – Sunset Lover: Petit Biscuit

4 – Just Breathe: Pearl Jam

5 – Free (Maya Jane Coles remix): Rudimental, ft. Emeli Sandé & Nas

6 – Fortunate Son: Creedence Clearwater Revival

7 – Basic Instinct (Thomas Jack remix): The Acid

8 – Apocalypse: Cigarettes After Sex

9 – Through My Ray-Bans: Eric Church

10 – Relax: Frankie Goes to Hollywood

11 – How Bad Do You Want It: Tim McGraw

12 – Walls: Kings of Leon

13 – Made for You: Jake Owen

14 – Piece of My Heart: Janis Joplin

15 – Death of Me: PVRIS

16 – Beast of Burden: The Rolling Stones

17 – Come Wake Me Up: Rascall Flatts

18 – True Colors: Cyndi Lauper

19 – Heaven Upside Down: Marilyn Manson

20 – Here Tonight: Brett Young

21 – My Guy: Mary Wells
22 – Late Night: Foals
23 – Here Comes the Shock: Green Day
24 – Broken Halos: Chris Stapleton
25 – All of It: Cole Swindell

Epilogue – You & Me (Flume remix): Disclosure
Bonus epilogue – One Man Guy: Rufus Wainwright

ACKNOWLEDGMENTS

To my dedicated beta readers, Elsie, Justine, and Rich. Thank you for sharing your precious feedback, loving my story, and cheering on my men as well as my secondary characters.

Also, now I know that some moves cannot be performed in a car... Without you, this book would not be what it is today. You rock!

To my scientist editor/my most avid reader/my nerdy friend/my soul sister from the other side of the ocean. You are truly unique, Sarah, and I owe you tons for putting your heart and soul into this book and my characters.

To two essential ladies, who were there for me, day(s) & night(s)! Rachel from BookJunky Author Services & Eileen Proksch from Germany! I owe you big time. ;)

To the inspiring Mitchell Wick—awesome DJ, breathtaking model and funny man—who introduced me to some of my favorite electro tunes.

A huge thanks to all the bloggers, readers and awesome social media communities for spreading the word. I am grateful that writing has also brought me new friends from all over the world.

THANKS TO ALL THE WRITERS who inspired me in the past and present and those who will do so in the future.

AND LAST BUT OBVIOUSLY NOT LEAST, I would like to congratulate my practically perfect in every way husband and my mini-me, who have been there every step of the way. Your understanding, faith and love contributed to making this book a reality. I'm so proud to have you in my life.

I love you.

ABOUT THE AUTHOR

HOPE IRVING **is a USA Today and Top 15 Amazon Bestselling author.**

She lives in Paris, France, with her supportive husband and creative teenage daughter. The French indie author spent a couple of years in Texas, where she earned her MBA. With many friends, relatives, and readers in the States, the US has a big place in her heart. Although French is her mother tongue, she chose to write her novels in English because it simply feels right for her characters.

Hope's suspenseful and complex love stories are modern fairytales that feature an unconventional Prince Charming and a headstrong heroine. A natural introvert, she enjoys tormenting her flawed characters with a hint of darkness and sometimes magical elements. Still, her heart melts when love conquers all. Her work has been described as "genre-defying," "refreshingly unique," and "an emotional rollercoaster read."

Learn more about Hope's life in Paris, her love of multi-layered, swoon-worthy heroes that don't play by the rules, and her book-loving world on her **website**. *To keep up with all the latest, follow Hope on social media or join* **Hope's mailing list** *for a FREE book as a welcome gift, exclusive book information and great deals.*

ALSO BY HOPE IRVING

CONTEMPORARY ROMANCE (M/F)

This or That is a standalone to *Omega Artist*
(A Cocky Hero Club Novel).

For a glimpse at Mike and Troy's future together and to visit some familiar faces, start *Omega Artist* today.

Omega Artist is an enemies-to-lovers, age gap emotional journey between a heavily tattooed broken man and a young and impulsive so-called feminist… unless she's simply trying to live as freely as a man in a patriarchal world.

I lured and tricked Tig into a random hookup on social media.

HE HAS NO CLUE he's anything but random to me. He has no clue we'll play by my rules. He has no clue I'll seduce him, then dump him because he deserves it. I refuse to allow manwhores like Tig de Luca to be praised and called Don Juan for collecting women, while I'm labeled as easy for test-driving the countless suitors selected by my old-fashioned father. I am a woman-empowering French influencer, and I'll teach the once famous tattoo artist a lesson. It's risk-free after all; I'm not into cocky alphas and crave a genuine connection.

I DIDN'T EXPECT the game to quickly escalate into steamy, intriguing, and witty conversations. I didn't expect our undeniable virtual chemistry to transfer to real life. I didn't expect to unearth the real man beneath the surface and guarded attitude. A widower who erected barriers to protect his wounded heart. A lonely thirty-something who's not the monster I believed him to be. An omega artist who's not my type, but that I share some unlikely affinities with.

STILL, WE BOTH WANT SOMETHING CASUAL that doesn't require a label. I can't let our infuriating attraction and astonishing compatibility overrule common sense. I'm on a mission after all. All good things must come to an end, right?

Except our ending was one I didn't see coming.

Buy it now on Amazon

Read for free on KU

OMEGA ARTIST is a standalone story inspired by Vi Keeland and Penelope Ward's Stuck-Up Suit.

It's published as part of the Cocky Hero Club world, a series of original works, written by various authors, and inspired by Keeland and Ward's New York Times bestselling series.

*Want to keep up with all of the new releases in Vi Keeland and Penelope Ward's Cocky Hero Club world? Make sure you sign up for the official **Cocky Hero Club newsletter** for all the latest on our upcoming books.*

CONTEMPORARY ROMANCE (M/F)

Discover *The Perry Witches' Legacy* series

(previously published as *The Black Angel Book Legend*.)

A second-chance forbidden love story about fate, secrets, and power.

A magical book. An evil organization. A forbidden love. Is the world as we know it about to collapse?

FOR CENTURIES, OUR STAR-CROSSED SOULS have tumbled through time, searching for each other and a second chance at our love story.

MORGANN, THE MONK. DEIRDRE, THE WITCH. And the ruthless evil organization we are up against to protect the most powerful spell ever cast. Now, I thought that finding my soulmate would be the hard part, but convincing Rose, her modern-day counterpart, of our past and the danger she's in will be the greatest challenge of my many lifetimes.

The series is complete & free to read with Kindle Unlimited: **Start today!**

Add to your TBR

NOW, WHO'S BRANDON BONER?

If you haven't met Mike's favorite adult movies producer, Brandon Boner yet, you should definitely check him out and read *Changing His Game* by the talented Justine Elvira. It's a contemporary romance (M/F); his story takes place prior to *This or That*.

I enjoyed this unique character so much that I asked for permission to borrow him.

Permission granted and I'm so proud!

CONTEMPORARY ROMANCE (M/F)

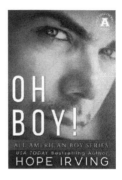

What started out as a battle for dominance changed when I realized my heart was on the line.

ARROGANT. SELF-CENTERED. OBNOXIOUS. Let's not forget ridiculously hot! I knew this guy would be trouble with a capital T. It doesn't take a rocket scientist to see that the famous calligrapher is confident in his own skin and my total opposite. Nathan Price...

MY SUMMER IN COLORADO is focused on work and music. There's no room to second-guess my safe choices because of his sweet talk. Thank goodness my favorite Guitar Hero is here to protect me and I gladly reciprocate.

NATHAN BELIEVES THAT I belong to another and offers his friendship, but the hunger in his eyes tells a different story. When we run into each other again, the playboy proves to be caring, patient, and understanding. My issues don't faze him. His obsessions don't scare me off. Am I seriously ready to risk everything in the name of attraction?

Oh boy!

Buy it now - Read for free on KU

Add it to your TBR

Oh Boy! is part of *The All-American Boy series*, a collection of interconnected stories written by various authors. Every story can be read as a standalone.

Welcome to Bear Creek, Colorado, an idyllic all-American mountain resort town and home of the USA Music Festival. Filled with summer love, country music and unexpected pleasures, this brand-new series of short contemporary stories will bring together a mix of summer fun and music with the backdrop of the Colorado Rocky Mountains.

The All-American Boy Series gives you a taste of 15 new books in a shared world experience. All books are standalone but may include cross-over in characters or scenes.

WANT FREEBIES AND NEWS FROM PARIS?

***Join* Hope's mailing list *for an exclusive ebook for free, book* information and great deals.**

Printed in Great Britain
by Amazon

81861428R00128